M000105503

"In *Coming Clean*, Betty Moffett pays homage to the power of story-telling, revealing the glimmer and grit that ripple beneath the stoic exterior of rural America. In prose that's as clean and inviting as a fresh-swept porch, Moffett lovingly chronicles the heart-swells and heartaches that make up a life well lived."
—Dean Bakopoulos, author, *Summerlong*

"I admire the charming, sometimes mischievous, restraint of the stories in *Coming Clean*. By holding back, they reveal life's mysteries all the more, and they pay homage to the laconic dignity of the people Betty Moffett writes about. The final story called 'Brothers' will break your heart in the best possible way."
—Ralph James Savarese, author, *Reasonable People* and *See It Feelingly*

"*Coming Clean* is a jewel box of a book: sparkling stories crafted by an artisan—some poignant, some funny, every one wise and word-smart—that span three generations of a quirky American family. Each story is graced by evanescent small beauties that make it as tactile as a kiss."
—David Campbell, author, *The Crystal Desert* and *A Land of Ghosts*

"Whether telling about small town mysteries, grade school epiphanies, or adolescent heart throbs, Betty Moffett's stories will enfold you in colorful fabrics woven of curiosity, emotion, exploration, and love. Some of the fabrics are rent, as families and communities can be, giving us glimpses of profound truths. These stories feel right, as only a gifted story teller can fashion them."
—Jonathan Andelson, Director of the Center for Prairie Studies at Grinnell College

"Betty Moffett's wisdom advances on noiseless footsteps to delight the receiver, like the gift of a pine cone in one of her stories. An acute observer of public follies and near-invisible triumphs, a gifted teller who shapes her tales with that rare craft that appears effortless, Moffett gives us a world of illuminated yet unsparing memory. The stories in *Coming Clean* circle back to dramatic moments re-told by a family down the generations, letting us see into their lives each time anew."
—Paula V. Smith, author, *The Painter's Muse*

"Betty Moffett represents what can be done by an author who brings great skill in fiction writing to the task of a memoir, giving memoir the sweet organization of fiction and fiction the authority of a lived truth. The Moffett we encounter in these works is both embedded in the cultures she describes and yet detached enough to see them as they are. As such, her view is realistic and unsparing, but also benevolent. The writing is pellucid and completely unpretentious. Moffett becomes a welcome partner from the first word on and we, turning the pages as fast as they permit, become her captives. This is a superb book that will enchant its every reader."
—Michael Cavanagh, author, *Professing Poetry: Seamus Heaney's Poetics*

"Betty Moffett convinces me that here we have a writer able to chronicle an interesting and productive life and to do so masterfully. I know that now I am appreciating the South of her youth and earlier adulthood to a greater degree, and although I've always lived in the Midwest, these accounts tune me in to some of the character types, rural landscapes and the small town life that we can easily take for granted."
—Tim Fay, *Wapsipinicon Almanac*

"With an easy grace, a ready wit, and an eye that misses nothing, Betty Moffett gives us stories that feel true to the lives they depict, true to each narrative moment. Time and again she turns just the right phrase, lands on the perfect word. Sometimes funny, sometimes wise, and sometimes both at once, the stories in *Coming Clean* linger in the mind as welcome company.
—Bryan Crockett, author, *Love's Alchemy*

Coming Clean

Stories

Betty Moffett

Ice Cube Press, LLC
North Liberty, Iowa, USA

For Sandy, of course,

and

For Alex, Lilly, and Eva

Coming Clean: Stories

The Store

The boy sat on the barrel in the store. And there he would stay, in his blue overalls worn thin, until his papa came back to fetch him. His papa wore overalls, too, the same soft blue, but he also wore a grey felt hat and his old suit coat. Across his bib was a gold watch chain.

His papa had told the boy to stay there on the barrel, so he would no more have moved than he would have sung and danced in the dusty street outside. He would no more have moved than he would have refused to go to Sunday school or to get up when his papa called him in the morning. He did what his papa told him.

He sat on the barrel and smelled the dust of the store, which was different somehow from the dust of the street—stiller, older, more fragrant. He was alone. The shopkeeper had gone to the back to help unload the supply wagon, or to the corner to talk with the other men about mules, horses, and the dry summer. He wondered if his papa would give him money for peppermint candy or for one of the thick brown cookies in the glass jar on the counter. Sometimes his father gave him money and sometimes his father bought a cigar for himself. The man never told the boy what to expect. The boy never asked.

He sat on the barrel and felt the splinters in the rim prick through his overalls and into the backs of his legs. He looked out the window, but he couldn't see much. Dust and dirt had collected around the edges of each pane until only the centers were clear. He waited for his papa. He was not unhappy sitting there.

The spring on the screen door screeched and a large man walked in. The buttonholes of his tight shirt were pulled almost round. He looked around for the storekeeper, saw but did not look at the boy. He didn't speak or nod. The boy was not surprised. He saw that the man was pleased to find the store empty. The man strolled to the grain bins and ran his hands through the oats and then through the corn, letting the grain run through his fingers, listening to the spilling sound, watching the dust rise. He took a bridle off a wooden peg and, frowning, looked at the way the blinkers were stitched to the leather cheek strap.

The boy understood that the man wanted to seem—even to him who did not matter—like someone who knew things, who judged.

Now the man was at the counter. He opened the cookie jar and looked inside, but he didn't touch the cookies. He ran two fingers across the fancy front of the cash register. Then he saw the small hole in the counter. The boy had seen his father stick the little end of a new cigar into the hole, and he remembered the sharp click and then the fresh, flat end of the cigar. Once, on his birthday, the storekeeper had taken him behind the counter and he had seen the pile of neat cigar tips that had fallen into the bucket beneath the hole.

Now he watched as the man put his hands, with the thumbs and fingers stretched apart, on either side of the hole. Then the man cupped his hands around the hole and tried to see down into it. He gave up, moved down to the end of the counter to look at the two kinds of tobacco, and then came back to the hole. It was a simple hole, bored into the dark, sticky wood of the counter with a brace and bit. The man tried again to see into the hole. His hands were flat on the counter, his head lower than his elbows and shoulders. The boy saw him straighten up and put the tip of his little finger inside the hole and he heard the snap, heard the man suck breath through his mouth. For the first time, then, the man looked at the boy, but quickly and still without speaking. Then he put his fist in his pocket, and, whistling, opened the screen door and went out into the street.

A Load Of Bricks

Wade was feeling pretty good for being handy and helping his little brother. Just yesterday, he had nailed one of his mama's empty wooden spools low on the frame of the screen door so Charles could get in by himself. His daddy was in the kitchen drinking buttermilk, and Wade heard him say, "Lula, that boy's right smart." In his ten years of living, Wade had had few compliments from his father, Wade Hampton Ferguson, who was known to all, including his wife, as Mr. Hamp. In fact, he couldn't remember one.

If his daddy was pleased with one of his children, he showed it by giving that child extra responsibility. So, that morning when he told Wade to hitch up Mike the mule and drive him to town for a load of bricks, Wade was proud. He meant to do this job so well that even Mr. Hamp, the world's best fault-finder, could find no flaw in his eldest son's work.

Wade and Mike were old acquaintances rather than friends. Together, they had turned many a long furrow in the red clay soil of the Ferguson farm, and Wade respected Mike's intelligence and strength. But he dreaded the mule's moods. Mike didn't kick, bite, or bolt. He just quit. Wade could twist, pull, whip, or beg, all with no results. He'd have to leave Mike standing in the field where he'd stopped, legs stiff as fence posts, and get his daddy, who made him feel the disgrace of asking for help. In heavy silence, the two would walk back to the field. Mr. Hamp would say, "Come up, mule," Mike would step out obediently, and Wade would take his place again between the plow handles. No word would pass between father and son.

So Wade watched for signs as he harnessed Mike. Were the muscles in his neck hard? Did he bunch his shoulders under the leather collar? The mule seemed peaceable, but Wade knew better than to trust him. Mike was a schemer, and Wade had an important job to do.

The load of bricks waiting in town would become the foundation for a new home for Wade and his family. For the first time, the Fergusons would be living in a house that belonged to them, one that the family, even the littlest ones, would help build. Wade imagined himself coming home with the weighty burden, sitting tall on the wagon seat like the general both he and his daddy were named for. He thought of the story his daddy once told him about General Hampton running the Confederate cavalry. Mr. Hamp's stories were good, but as rare as his compliments. He held that wasting words, like wasting money, was a sin.

Just two days earlier, Mr. Hamp and the hired man had finished a new wide bed for the wagon, made out of pine boards from the straight trees in the woodlot. Beads of sap circled the knots in the rough-cut boards, and the smell of resin was sweet in the air. Mike backed willingly into the traces, and Wade made his voice deep like his daddy's to say, "Come up, mule."

Mike seemed to appreciate the downward tilt of the red road, and the five miles to town passed quickly. Wade kept the reins loose and his hat tipped forward, so he felt rather than saw the sun climb above the trees. He sang, in his pretty good tenor voice:

Further along, we'll know all about it.

Further along, we'll understand why.

He might have dozed, but the idea of being seen asleep on the job, and the certainty that his father would hear of it, kept his back straight as a soldier's. When the road dropped sharply just before the feed store appeared, the boy was ready for Mike's usual trick of swerving back and forth over the ruts. But the mule simply shifted his weight, making his back legs shorter and his front legs longer, and walked with small steps to the bottom of the hill.

Wade wrapped Mike's tie rope twice around the hitching rail that marked the south end of Main Street and started toward the store. Then he turned back, put a double knot in the rope, and tried to catch Mike's eye, but the mule's lids were drooping and his ears were in neutral.

Inside the store, Mr. Womble called out, "Well hey, young Wade. Mr. Hamp's got him a hand now, for sure, don't he? We'll load them bricks soon as I add up these figures." Wade was glad to wait in the dusty cool of the store. The sway-backed shelves held cans of Vienna sausage and peaches, jack knives, nails, chewing tobacco and snuff, and bolts of cloth. He wasn't finished looking when Mr. Womble slapped his hands twice on his hips and said,

"All right now, boy, the sooner we start, the sooner we'll be done. Ain't that right? Bring that old wagon round the back here."

As Wade lined mule and wagon up beside the loading dock, he realized Mr. Womble had already said more words to him than his daddy would use in a week, and he thought less of the storekeeper for it.

Mike stood patiently while man and boy stacked the bricks in the wagon. At first, Mr. Womble gave advice. "Don't slam 'em now, else they'll crack," and "Line 'em up real straight." But soon the dark, rough bricks passed in a wordless rhythm from hand to hand until the wagon held the load—wide, level, and six bricks deep.

"Wanna co-cola?" Mr. Womble asked. Wade said. "Yes sir." He understood that the ribbed green bottle with ice sliding down its sides was a kind of praise from the storekeeper. So was his silence as they sat together on the loading dock with their sweet, stinging drinks.

Then Mr. Womble clapped his hands, rubbed them together, and said, "Well, fun's over. You and that old mule better get on back to the farm. Say hey to your mama and daddy, hear?"

Wade would have liked to keep the bottle, but Mr. Womble took it back inside the store. Before he climbed on the wagon, he stood for a minute at Mike's head. He didn't think of patting the animal, but in his pleasure at a job well done, he said, "All right, mule, we're going home." Mike stood with one leg cocked, looking off to the side at nothing in particular.

At Wade's "Come up," the mule took two steps, and stopped. Through the reins, Wade could feel Mike's displeasure at the heavy load. Clearing his throat to lower his voice, he said again,

"Come up, mule." He knew Mr. Womble was watching. When Mike leaned into the breast band and the wagon began to move again, Wade let out his breath and watched Mike's shoulder muscles roll under his skin with each step. And then the road began to rise and the mule quit pulling.

First, Wade made sure he was out of sight of the store. Then he slapped the reins hard on Mike's rump. He slapped again and yelled the mule's name, but his voice came out high and tight. Mike's body had lost all forward thrust. He stood with his weight perfectly distributed among his legs. He could stand there, Wade knew, all day.

When Wade climbed down and went to face the mule, Mike turned his ears forward and gazed over the boy's head. Pulling on the reins was useless—the mule just made his neck long. Useless, too, were the rotten pine branch Wade broke over Mike's rear and the two swear words he knew. And he didn't want to make Mike really mad. He squatted down beside the wagon, hoping, praying even, that nobody would come by and offer help to Mr. Hamp's oldest boy. He could hear the stories they'd tell, all beginning, "That sorry Ferguson boy." The sun was behind the wagon, and the shadows pointed west.

One of the pieces of rotten branch was leaning on the wagon wheel. Wade picked it up and then saw another close by. Standing, he began to gather dry sticks. Then he stopped to look at Mike again. The mule's only move had been to cock his right hip and rest the tip of that hoof on the ground. He looked comfortable. "All right, then," Wade said, and began to place the sticks in a circle, each one pointing inward, under the mule's belly. He kept a constant eye on Mike's back feet. Mule kicks, he knew, were the very worst kind. After topping off the branches with dry leaves and twigs rubbed to a powder between his palms, he fished a red-headed match from the bib pocket of his overalls, struck it on the side of the wagon, and set his fire. Mike smelled it first and then felt the heat on his belly. When he flattened his ears and lunged forward, Wade grabbed for the reins, imagining a runaway mule and flying bricks. But Mike moved just enough to put the hot fire squarely under the wide bed of the wagon. Then he stopped.

Dropping to his knees, Wade could see the soft beads of sap pop and flame. Then a blue-red circle began to spread across the pine boards. Smoke stung his eyes. "Papa," he thought, and then he tore a green-needled bough off the nearest tree and scattered the fire. Running from one side to the other, Wade scrubbed the hot center of the wagon's underside with more pine boughs. Then he rolled under the wagon and mashed out the last sparks with the heels of his hands. He made sure his feet were facing Mike, just in case the mule ever moved again. Face and hands black, eyes watering, he rolled back out and sat beside his load of bricks.

"Well," he said out loud.

When he looked up, the sun was touching the tallest trees, and he was out of ideas. The only thing he could think to do was just ordinary. He climbed up on the wagon, put his hat on his head, and said, "Come up, mule." And Mike came up, moving the wagon steadily up the hill and down the road.

Watching Mike strain against the harness, Wade thought maybe he should offer up a little prayer of thanks. But then he remembered Mr. Hamp, who'd be waiting at the barn like God on Judgment Day. Maybe he'd just keep quiet. Maybe Papa wouldn't notice. But no. First he'd smell the char, then he'd squat down and look under the wagon, then…. Wade let that thought run out. Then he had another, different thought. He had been smart to build that fire. Never mind that Mike was smarter. And he hadn't run begging for help. And he'd done his job, though Papa wouldn't have to look far to find fault.

And someday, it would make a real good story.

The Last Whipping

Charles Worth Ferguson wasn't worth much, he figured. He was Mr. Hamp and Miss Lula's third child. Before him had come a girl, sweet Rosser, and that smart boy, Wade Hampton, named after Papa. So, right from the start, Charles was bound to be a repeat of something. Papa helped him remember that by calling Wade and Rosser by their names but addressing his second son as "Boy."

"I've called you once, Boy," Papa would say. "Get up or get a whipping."

Since smart and sweet were already taken, and he had no talent for either, Charles worked out that he could be strong. When he was still doing baby chores, slopping hogs and feeding chickens, he heard his father praise a neighbor boy for carrying a bale of hay under each arm, and Charles willed his own strength to come up in him. After Papa set him to plowing and milking, he felt his legs, arms, and back grow hard. His thoughts grew hard, too.

He had to be careful of his mama. His mama made him soft. He liked to watch her peel apples. The red skin came off in a long, unbroken strip. And he thought her braided hair was pretty. His mama called him by his name, and, when they were alone, she told him he was her boy. There was a difference in his father's 'Boy' and his mother's 'My boy.' So he kept away from her mostly, but sometimes he couldn't help trying to please her. Once, he heard her say she wished somebody would get rid of the two tomcats that yowled outside the house in the night. He caught the cats, one black and one yellow, and, ignoring the furrows they clawed in his arms, tied their tails together and flung them over the clothes line.

Right away, he knew he'd done wrong. His mother came to the window and began to cry. The cats' screams brought Papa up from the milk barn. He saw the bloodied cats and made a sound that might have been a laugh. He made Charles cut the cats down, then opened the door to the smokehouse, jerked an old razor strop off its nail, took his son behind the smokehouse, and whipped him.

Before he was eight, Charles had decided he would no longer beg or cry during Papa's whippings. By the time he was eleven, he could take a beating without a sound, and he scorned the others—there were five more children after him—when they sobbed under Papa's stern sense of justice.

The family's dog, Rex, was more hired hand than pet. He earned his keep by bringing in the cows and catching barn rats. Charles thought Rex was a good worker and approved of the fear the dog inspired in the dairy herd, who dreaded his quick teeth. Sometimes, Charles would push his hand down in Rex's ruff to

12

feel the combined heat of the dog's body and the warm sun on his fur. But the evening Rex failed to bring Crip, the best milker, up from the pasture, Charles cut a hickory switch and broke it over the dog's back. For days afterward, Rex wouldn't let Charles put his hand on him, and Charles made no move to regain the animal's trust.

Both Mr. Hamp and Miss Lula wanted their brood educated, so Charles walked to school with Wade and Rosser and the rest. He didn't mind. The books mattered little to him, but he liked escaping from farm work, and he liked sports. Tall and work-toughened, in the fall, he excelled at football. When spring came, the baseball flew off his powerful bat. Once, Papa, who sat on the school board, was there when Charles hit a homerun. But best of all was the in-between season, when he could sit in the warm gym and watch the girls play basketball. Some of them looked kind, like his mama. Some tied their hair back with blue ribbons, to match their uniforms. As they stood with their backs to the wood stove that heated one corner of the gymnasium, Charles noticed the delicate diamond shapes in their winter-dry shins. Some of the girls smiled at him. Sometimes, he smiled back.

On the morning after his fifteenth birthday, Papa called up the dark stairs, "You all get up and start milking." Charles lay listening to the others' moans and rustlings. He was tired. He had spent the day before plowing behind Mike, the mule, stopping only to pull up the white rocks that made the plow buck, and then pitch them to the edge of the field. He barely stayed awake to eat the cake his mama served him after supper. When Wade rolled out of the bed they shared, Charles turned over and pulled up the quilt.

"You lay there, you'll get the reins," Wade said. But Charles closed his eyes.

When he opened his eyes again, his father stood over him. "Come to the smokehouse, Boy," he said.

Charles's mama stopped kneading biscuits and watched him walk through the kitchen and out into the dim day. Wade was right, Charles knew. This time, Papa would use the bridle reins. The razor strop hurt, but the reins drew blood.

Back of the smokehouse, Papa was waiting. "Pull up your shirt, Boy," he said. Charles reached down to do as he was told. But when Papa raised his arm with the reins in his fist, Charles turned and grabbed his father's wrist. Their arms made a steeple above their heads. Neither spoke. The two strong men leaned into each other until the older man's arm began to tremble. When his father finally dropped the reins, Charles bent down, picked them up and handed them back to him. The two looked at each other until Charles turned his head and walked away. He waited till he was milking the first cow to cry.

Dan

Uncle Charles ran a small dairy farm on the 250 acres his father had left to his brood of six children. The other five were scattered around the state, but often came back to the home place on weekends, and then the old house smelled of frying chicken and simmering collard greens and Pyrex pans of peach cobbler baking in the oven. After dinner, people sat on the screen porch and told stories and laughed. Uncle Charles mostly listened, and smiled, sometimes. He liked these weekends, and made sure the old place looked good—lawn mowed, fences tight. When my parents had been too busy to get "back home" for a while, Uncle Charles would call and say, "When you all coming?" He never sounded sad or needy, but my daddy could hear the lonely in his brother's voice, and the next Friday we'd pack our bags and head for the red clay foothills and the Ferguson farm.

I loved those visits, loved the food and the quilts on the iron beds, loved Aunt Nina, who read *Black Beauty* to me—again and again and again—and my boy cousins, who teased and spoiled me. But I loved Uncle Charles best.

He wasn't the easiest person to love. He didn't wait for me to catch up or carry me across the creek on his back. But when he stood up from the dinner table, pointed at me, and said, "Want to come help with chores?" I hurried to join him. Of course I was no help at all, but he let me think I was.

We'd walk out to the big three-story barn my granddaddy had built, me half running to match his long-legged strides, and climb to the second floor hayloft. The rungs on the wooden ladder had felt so many feet, they dipped in the middle and were as smooth as the oiled leather in the tack room. I couldn't have gotten a splinter in my hands if I'd tried. Not that Uncle Charles ever cautioned me against that danger. He paid me the great compliment of assuming I could take care of myself.

He made one exception. As we threw hay down to the cows waiting expectantly below, he pointed out that if I was foolish enough to fall, Toby the bull would be pleased to do me harm.

My uncle had a way with animals, and it was not a gentle way. He never scratched the ears of Rex, the half-shepherd dog who helped him round up the cows, or rubbed the kind faces of his Jersey milkers. He fed them, treated their ailments, made sure they could get to the creek for water, and in return, he expected—demanded—obedience, not affection.

And he got it. Rex came running, body low to the ground, when Uncle Charles whistled, sat at his hand signal, and brought in the herd at the order "Get 'em." The cows walked obligingly into their assigned stalls and waited for the milking machines.

Toby, though, was less compliant, and the ongoing contest between the bull and Uncle Charles frightened and fascinated me.

When we moved the hay bales to the loft door (well, Uncle Charles moved them, I got to cut the string), the cows raised their hopeful brown eyes and mooed. Toby, a wide-chested, wide-browed Hereford who still had his horns, pawed the ground and snorted, sliming the ring in his nose. Once, when Toby had broken through a fence, I saw my uncle grab that ring in the bull's nose and twist it till the animal fell to its knees; then he led a chastened Toby back into the pasture. And I saw promise, not submission, in the bull's eyes. My uncle kept Toby because he produced good calves, but also because he had gumption. My uncle had no time for spiritless animals. But there was a limit: he would not put up with insubordination, and no animal that threatened to hurt his pride stayed long on the Ferguson farm.

Which is why, according to my aunts, their brother didn't stay married. I have only a vague memory of dark-haired Linda, who was Charles's wife for seven months. I remember how fine they looked together one Saturday night when they were dressed up to go out, and soon after, she was gone for good. Aunt Nina said that Linda thought she could put some polish on Charles—clean up his grammar and his work boots and take him to swanky restaurants. And he tried, for a while. But then Linda began to suggest that the Fergusons weren't as good as her people, that they lacked "breeding." When she referred to her in-laws as "hill billies," Charles didn't yell or slam around the house. He just stopped speaking to her. And pretty soon, she packed up and left, and nobody talked about her anymore.

Uncle Charles' pride wasn't the bragging kind. If not for Daddy's stories, I would never have known that my uncle had been considered the strongest man in the county: he could lift more bales of hay, carry more sacks of feed, and dig more post holes than any man for thirty miles around. And—and it hurt my father, a good rider himself, to say this—his brother was still the county's best horseman. In his prime, my father told me, Charles Ferguson and his cronies, male and female, could ride horses all night—through the woods, up the red clay hills, across the rocky creek beds. When dawn came and the others went home to their beds, Charles unsaddled his horse, rubbed him down, gave him hay and oats, and then headed for the fields to plow, haul rocks, and cut timber. This impossible regimen seemed to suit him, largely because my uncle's great and constant love was horses.

The fact that, from my earliest memory, I shared that passion was, I think, the main reason my uncle tolerated my company. He always had horses in the barn. Some he bought to sell or trade, but three were always there—two tall sorrel saddle-breds (Lady Flash for my father, Lady Margaret for my uncle) and one impossibly big Percheron named Dan.

I was completely happy when I could watch my father and my uncle—both black-haired, both handsome—ride their horses at a full rack down the driveway, the horses' iron shoes making sparks in the gravel. Then, my father would dismount, fling me up on his saddle, swing up behind me, and head off across the county with my uncle at our side.

The two Ladys were highbred and skittish, and ready to spook at anything—a paper bag, a coil of fence wire, pigs—especially pigs. When a big muddy sow suddenly appeared in a neighbor's pasture, grunting and snuffling, her piglets running between her feet, I could feel Lady Flash crouch and make a right angle of her body. But just before she jumped three feet sideways, Daddy tightened his arm around my waist, laughed, and scolded his horse gently. Like his brother, he preferred his animals spirited.

And that's why Uncle Charles decided to sell tall, red and handsome Kingdom, a Tennessee Walker he'd bought recently at an auction. King had the looks of a horse that would fit in on the farm, but riding him for a week had revealed that he had no pep, no courage. So my uncle had invited two prospective buyers to come to Sunday dinner and take a look at King. In fact, J. R. and Nancy Ferguson were Uncle Charles' second cousins. Nancy, who ran a riding school, thought King might make a good, steady mount for her beginners. I could tell right away that Nancy (who was married-in, not blood kin) made the decisions, and I was glad she seemed to like King's looks and manners.

After fried chicken, milk gravy, turnip greens, and coconut cake, Uncle Charles led the horse up from the barn. He'd offered to ride King around the yard to show off his gaits. He told the horse to 'park out,' and King responded quickly by moving his front feet forward, bringing his body closer to the ground so my uncle could mount easily. But when he stepped into the stirrup, the saddle slipped a little and he knew that King, as many horses do, had puffed up his belly to keep the cinch from being pulled too tight. Uncle Charles's face flushed. The horse had embarrassed him—and maybe queered the sale. He balled up his fist and hit King sharply in the stomach. The horse released his breath and my uncle was about to tighten the cinch, when Nancy, who may or may not have been five feet tall, marched up to my uncle, swung her arm back, and hit him just above his belt. "How does it feel?" she demanded.

I closed my eyes. I knew my uncle was going to hit this tiny woman and probably kill her. But when I looked, he was making a little bow. "I admire your spunk, ma'am," he told her.

Nancy bought the horse. Uncle Charles was pleased with the sale, but he never invited the couple to another Sunday dinner. The big horse and the little woman had hurt his pride.

If Lady Margaret was Uncle Charles's convertible sports car, Dan, the black Percheron stallion, was his muscle, his bulldozer, and his wrecking ball. Oh, my uncle used his red International Harvester rig for the long, boring jobs like planting and harvesting corn, but for the dramatic stuff like pulling down trees or raising the thick iron dinner bell to its new scaffold, he always harnessed Dan. I loved to see that horse come out of his stall, wearing only his leather halter, picking up his hubcap-sized feet, nodding his huge head up and down as if to say, "Let's do it." He was always bigger than I remembered.

Only rarely did Uncle Charles put me up on Dan's back. First, that back was so broad that my legs stuck out in an awkward split; and second, Dan was not a pet, not a decorative Sunday riding horse. But he was beautiful. His black hide shone like oil, his mane was long and heavy enough to hide in. I wondered how it was that my uncle, a thin, pale dwarf beside this giant horse, had convinced Dan that he, the man, was the master. I had seen Dan shiver when my uncle spoke sharply to him, and I had seen him give all his great strength when Uncle Charles "gee'd" him into a pull. I decided I didn't want to know the history of their arrangement.

One Sunday after church, Uncle Charles and I found ourselves alone in the big house. My parents had gone to visit the Kelloggs, who were restoring the old mill, and my aunts had packed up their chicken pie, pound cake, and families and headed back to their homes. My uncle and I were comfortable together. He thumbed through *Progressive Farmer*; I read the Sunday funnies. We didn't talk and we both kept an eye on the old Regulator clock. When it struck one, we'd get up and start the chores.

Just when the clock was clearing its throat to strike, we heard someone knocking on the front door. I knew it had to be a stranger, because everyone we knew came around to the screen porch. Curious, we opened the door. A man wearing a tan overcoat and pale leather shoes touched the brim of his felt hat and said, "Sorry to bother you good folk, but I have foolishly gotten my car stuck in the ditch across from your house. And I was wondering, Sir, if you had a tractor that could pull me out."

Everything about the man—manners, clothes, speech—said "rich." And I could feel my uncle's resistance, almost read his thoughts: City man. He'll have a fancy car. Looking to hire a poor hillbilly farmer to get him out of the mud so he won't have to get those pretty shoes dirty.

What he said was, "I'll help any man who needs it. My tractor's broke down [I knew it wasn't] but I've got an old horse who might could do the job."

"A horse? Well, I don't know...," the man began. Then he looked at his thick gold watch and said, "I'd be grateful for any help you can offer."

As the man walked back to his car, Uncle Charles and I went to the barn for Dan. I had a dozen questions: Why did you say that about the tractor? Why did you call Dan "old"? Why.... But I knew I should keep quiet and keep up.

Dan was delighted to see us. When Uncle Charles snapped a lead rope on his halter and led him out of his stall, he snorted lightly and nodded his huge head. As always, I wondered how

21

any living thing could be that big, that beautiful. My uncle took his time. He brushed Dan's already glistening back, straightened his mane, cleaned his hooves. Then he fastened the complicated pulling harness on his stallion. I understood then that Uncle Charles was going to do something I'd never seen him do before: He was going to show off for this rich city man. I crossed my fingers hard, hoping that Dan wouldn't embarrass my uncle.

The sleek yellow Buick was tilted up at an almost comical angle. Its back wheels were all but invisible, sunk into the red clay of the ditch. The man, who'd been sitting behind the steering wheel, took another quick look at his watch, then, smiling, stepped out of his car, his shoes, like his car wheels, sinking into the slick clay. "By the way," he said, "I'm Ned Daniels, and from the name on your mailbox, I assume you're Mr. Ferguson. That's a splendid animal you have there, Sir."

"My daddy was Mr. Ferguson," Uncle Charles said, hooking the heavy chain to the front axle of the car. The Buick and the man's courtesy had made my uncle abrupt, nearly rude. "Better stand back," he said. "Don't want to get mud on your coat."

At the "gee-up" command, Dan began to pull. The car didn't move. "Gee, Dan," Uncle Charles said again, and slapped the long reins on the horse's back. Dan squatted on his haunches, straining forward. I could see the muscles swell in his neck. Still nothing.

"Sir," Mr. Daniels said, "I don't want that horse to hurt himself. Looks like this is a job for a machine."

"Gee up," said my uncle, but Dan no longer needed urging. He had found his own pride now, and he'd burst his big heart before he'd quit this job. I heard Dan gulp air, saw ragged ribbons of sweat run down his sides, saw his huge hooves slip in the mud. And, with a slurping sound, the car popped out of the ditch.

Dan stood, head lowered, shaking a little. Uncle Charles put his hand on the horse's back, and left it there.

"My God—sorry, Miss—I never saw anything like that," Mr. Daniels almost shouted. "I never thought he'd do it. It was grand. Grand!"

Then he took out his wallet, removed a twenty-dollar bill, and held it out to my uncle.

No, I thought. *That's wrong. He'll hate that.*

And, "I'm not your hired hand, Mister. I don't take money for doing a favor for a man in need." I heard the pride and anger in my uncle's voice.

"Mr. Ferguson," the man answered, "I'm not offering to pay a gentleman for rescuing me. This money is for the pleasure of watching that big horse pull." After what seemed like a long time, my uncle and the rich man shook hands.

When we came to visit Uncle Charles again, he and I climbed the ladder to the dusty, sweet-smelling hayloft and fed the cows and Toby as usual. We gave the Ladys their oats and listened to them chew. Then, we went to Dan's stall. Dan greeted us with an expectant "huh-huh-huh" and nods of his great black head. He was wearing his familiar leather halter, but now, just below each ear, I saw a shiny concho the size of a Mason jar lid. I remembered the twenty dollars, and I looked at my Uncle Charles. He smiled.

"Ten dollars apiece," he said. "They're real silver."

And that's the closest I ever came to hearing my uncle brag.

Neighbors

Donny Ross and I were best friends, but our friendship was doomed. When you're five years old, you can't be best friends without seeing each other every day, and my mama and I were about to move to be closer to my daddy, who was in the army.

For as long as I could remember, I had lived across the Wide Yard from Donny. We played together during the warm blue-sky days, and separated at dusk, before tiredness made us fuss. We meant it when we sat in the silver maple's branches and said to each other, "I wishened you lived at my house," but I think we knew our arrangement was better.

My mama and I lived upstairs in the big house, above Sue Ross and her mama, Ella. Sue was six and a little bossy, but not mean. The only time she ever hurt me was when she brushed my hair. Both of our daddies were off at the war. Mama and Ella talked about the Germans and Japanese, who were bad, and our allies, who were good. We had strong pacts with those friends, they explained. I thought they were saying "packs," so when they said these friends would always stand by us, I pictured wolves or lions, and felt very safe indeed.

Donny lived with his brother, Randy, and sister, Jenny, and their parents, Randolph and Jennifer. The Ross children were cousins, but they never made me feel like an outsider. I knew Donny would have saved my life before his brother's because he told me so. The five of us children ran back and forth across the Wide Yard as naturally as the tide I'd seen on the North Carolina beach. I had thought we would run free like that forever.

When the war ended, and everyone sang "Let freedom ring," I was glad—mostly because everybody else was, and also because my daddy, who I liked but didn't know very well, would be coming to live with us again. But that was before I knew we were moving to a little town called Southwood, where both my parents would be teachers. Now, when Donny and I said "I wishened you lived at my house," we were serious, and sad.

And then a trailer sat in the driveway, hitched to our green Ford. Everybody helped bring our belongings down the stairs, and Daddy told them how to pack so things wouldn't rattle. He put my doll's bed on the upside-down seat of a chair to keep it safe. I told Donny goodbye.

Our new house was all ours, and tables and toys found their places inside. One morning, Mama took me outside to meet the children who lived next door. Their parents had already come to see us. Miss Helen May was big and soft with a pretty, downy face and a loud laugh. She had made fried chicken and a lemon meringue pie. Mr. Stub May was bald and the town mayor. He carried the chicken.

When Mama and I came over to their yard, the three May children stood in a line. Buddy, the oldest, and Sister, the youngest, were short like their daddy. Preston was tall and almost fat, like his mama.

"Hey," Sister said.

"Good morning," my mama said. "We're your new neighbors. I'm Miss Jane, and this is Betty." I was glad she didn't say, "I know you all will be friends."

I thought that was enough for one day, but Mama let go of my hand, left me standing there, and went back to poke in the flowers by our front door.

"Hey Betty," Sister said. She made my name sound like "Biddy." Then she walked around me to look at the back of my dress. Preston drew a line in the grass with his foot and said, "This is where our yard starts." After that, all three children went back to their house. Sister turned around to wave, but Buddy pushed her arm down. My daddy didn't usually talk much about the war, but he had told me about allies and boundaries. I knew that Preston had just made a boundary. And I was pretty sure allies didn't have boundaries.

My feet felt stuck to the ground. I couldn't cross Preston's line. It might as well have been fire, or poison. I couldn't go back to Mama. She was a mama, not a friend. I went to the sidewalk in front of our house and jumped the cracks, too sad even to wish for Donny.

After breakfast the next day, I went out the back door to watch Daddy. He was building me a swing set out of silver pipes. And there was Sister, building a stick house right where our yards came together. She had marked out two rooms, and she handed me some sticks. "Here's the kitchen and the bedroom," she said. "You make a great big dining room, and I'll make a porch."

I thought I'd kept a lookout for Buddy and Preston, but they surprised me anyway. In a minute, they'd dragged their feet through our house and wrecked all but the kitchen. Sister yelled, "You mean old things," but they didn't even look at her. Then my tall daddy stood up and said, "Here now." He could make the whole world stop by saying those words.

"Get home," Buddy told Sister, and he and Preston moved pretty fast back across their yard with Sister between them.

I started to fix the stick house, but it wasn't fun anymore, so I watched Daddy saw seats for the swings. That night he told me that sometimes countries like America and Germany fought each other because they lived by different rules. He made it seem like he was telling me about the war, but I knew he was talking about me and the May children.

Saturdays, I listened to Buster Brown on the radio, and this time, I was especially sad when it was over. Then I heard a noise and looked out the window. Sister was riding her tricycle on the sidewalk in front of our house. She had a card fastened to the front wheel with a clothespin. When it hit the spokes, it made a fluttering sound. She rode back and forth, back and forth, stopping at each end to lift up her trike and turn it around. After a while, I went out and sat on our front steps. Sister peddled up to me and asked, "You got one of these?"

"Uh-huh," I said. "Mine's in the garage. It's not unpacked yet." I wasn't going to ride it until I knew where my sidewalk ended and the Mays' sidewalk began.

"Well, my brothers are playing Rolly Bat in the back yard. Let's go play with them."

I shook my head.

"Come on," she said, getting off her trike and heading it in the direction of her house. "Mama said she'd beat the hell out of them if they weren't nice to me."

I'd heard those kinds of words before when grownups talked about our country's enemies, but nobody had ever said it about anybody I knew. I was scared but interested. If Miss Helen was going to beat the hell out of Buddy and Preston, I wanted to see it happen.

Sister left her tricycle with its front wheel butting against the big magnolia tree in front of their house, and the two of us walked around to their backyard. I made sure I could still see my house.

Buddy was batting. He stood on home base, an old tee-shirt, tossed the ball up and hit it out to Preston, the fielder. "Mama said you had to let me play," Sister told her older brother. He didn't answer.

"You get two more hits," Preston said to Buddy, then threw the ball hard to his brother. Sister and I might as well have been weeds or gnats, but I liked being the same as somebody.

"Okay, that's two. My bat," Preston said, trotting in. His cheeks bounced when he ran.

"Nah," Buddy said. "That last one was just a little dink. I get another turn."

"Hell you do," and Preston grabbed the bat from his brother.

Buddy put his fists up, pretending to be a boxer, but when Preston raised the bat like a weapon, Buddy said, "Well, be that way," and added, much softer, "Cheater."

I was kind of glad that the two brothers were mad at each other. At least they'd forgotten to be mad at me.

italics for emphasis

"Mama *said*," Sister repeated, and Buddy growled, "Well, you and that girl get out in the field then. I'll play pitcher."

That girl? I knew he knew my name.

The first hit came toward Sister. She stopped the ball with her feet, and then ran forward with it.

"Stop, Stupid," said Buddy. "You have to roll from where you pick it up." But Sister stood her ground, and when she rolled the ball, it bumped the fat part of the bat.

"My turn, my turn," Sister skipped toward home base.

"It is not. That was my first hit, and anyway, the ball never touched the bat."

"Mama!" Sister screamed.

"Al-right, Ba-by," Buddy said, making every syllable sound mean.

The bat was almost too heavy for Sister to lift, and she had to choke up to the top of the tape, but on her third swing, the ball puttered right out to me. *Maybe she meant to. Maybe we're friends,* I thought. I almost said, "Thanks," and my roll was straight and true. But Sister nudged the bat with her foot, and the ball rolled past.

"No fair," I said. Buddy and Preston ran up, and once again I faced a line of May children.

"Are you calling our sister a cheater?" Preston demanded. He picked up the end of the bat, but left the tip resting on the ground.

I wanted to yell for my mama, but I knew better. I wanted to cry, and I wanted to run. I had to make myself walk back to my house even though my face was hot and the whole back of me was crawling with ants.

For a while, I stuck close to home. My herd of plastic horses ran and grazed on our new green living room rug. My Sparkle Plenty doll wore all her outfits. I thought of calling Donny on the phone, but there was nothing good to say.

I'd just started looking at the *Bobbsey Twins* books that Mama'd brought me from the library. Their arrangement looked pretty good. Nan and Bert and Freddy and Flossie lived in a family of friends. I heard a knock on the door, opened it, and there was Sister.

"Want to come to my house?" she asked. "Mama's making sugar cookies."

I really didn't want to go, and I really did. So, when my mama, who'd heard us from the kitchen, said, "Go on, Betty, that sounds like fun," I felt both happy and betrayed.

We crossed the invisible line Preston had drawn with his foot, and I felt electricity in my ankles. I turned around to look for Mama's face at the kitchen window, but the sun made it a blank orange square. I remembered Daddy telling Mama about soldiers who went into enemy territory and were never seen again.

But the Mays' house was full of cookie smell. Miss Helen said, "Well hey, Betty," and handed Sister and me each a little ball of raw dough. When Sister popped hers in her mouth, I did the same, and I could taste the smell of the house.

We leaned our elbows on the counter to get as close as we could to the pan of sweet warm circles Miss Helen took out of the oven. She gave us glasses of milk and put a plate of cookies between us.

"You have one and I'll have one, then you have one and I'll have one. You first." Sister was being nice, but I was cautious. I'd seen how quickly she could change.

Then Preston strolled in, feet bare, hands in his pockets. I sat still. He made his fingers snap like a hungry mouth toward our plate of cookies. Sister squealed. Preston grinned at his mama, who grinned back and gave him his own cookies. Then Preston looked at me and said, "When's your daddy gonna finish those swings?" I couldn't hear any meanness in those words, so I said, "Probably next week." He said, "Good." It was cheerful in the kitchen.

Sister and I played dolls and bob jacks on the floor beside her bed until Miss Helen said, "Time for lunch, Carol Ann." I thought she was talking to somebody else until Sister stood up and said, "You have to go home now. I'll come see you tomorrow." I'd been pushed out of the Mays' pack again, but not so roughly this time.

In the long, warm days of that summer, the circle around my neighbors softened, sometimes disappeared. Now and then I forgot about the line in the grass. We children, and sometimes our whole families, moved from one yard to the other for barbeque picnics. Mama and Miss Helen shelled peas together in the magnolia's shade. Buddy, Preston, Sister, and I managed to take turns on my new swings. I got used to the Mays' roughness and no longer expected bloody murder when Buddy chased Preston, yelling, "If I catch you, you're dead," or when Miss Helen called her children to dinner with "Get in here, you damn young-uns." But I couldn't find the comfortable easiness I had felt with the

Ross cousins. The May children didn't wishen I lived with them, and I didn't wishen they lived with me.

It was late August, and the air was like wet Kleenex. School would start in a week, and we were glad—and sorry—to give up the sweet monotony of summer. Sister and I would both be in first grade, but not in the same class. I would have welcomed her support if I thought I could depend on it. Mama said she was sure I'd find brand new friends quick, but when I asked her to promise, she wouldn't.

It was too hot for Rolly Bat, too hot to work some more on the swimming pool we'd started to dig in the May's backyard, too hot even to swing. Sis (we girls had decided to shorten her name) and I were watching our dolls take a nap in a brand-new stick house under the magnolia. Mr. Stub had told Buddy and Preston they had to pick up the egg-shaped seed pods the tree was always dropping. "Hanganeggs," the boys called them, a mushy mouthing of "hand grenades."

At first, they tossed them at each other, breaking off the stems and counting "three-two-one" before the throw. Then they bombed our sleeping dolls. Inevitably, Sis and I became targets. For a while, the boys threw underhand, and the pods were more a house-cleaning nuisance than a danger. Then, inevitably, Preston threw a hard pitch that caught his sister in the ear. And inevitably, she screamed and fell down. Dots of blood came on the side of her face. She looked murdered. When Miss Helen looked out the door, the boys scattered. My doll and I, sole survivors, headed home.

After lunch, I wandered outside again. All three May children were in their yard, drugged into peace by the heat. Sis waved

32

me over. Buddy and Preston were squatting on the porch steps trying to make an old pocket knife stick in the hard dirt. Sis and I rolled down the windows of the Mays' Chevy and sat in the front seat. We were going to Florida for a vacation. She was driving, and I could see the orange medicine Miss Helen had painted on her ear.

When Buddy went inside for a drink, Preston came over and climbed in behind us.

"Think you're going somewhere?" he asked.

"Yeah, Florida, to see the alligators," Sis answered.

I thought her friendliness was strange. Then I saw her push in the cigarette lighter. She put her hands back on the steering wheel and turned it back and forth, making a humming noise for the motor.

"You can't even reach the gas pedal," Preston said. On the word "pedal," the lighter popped out. Sis grabbed it, turned in her seat, and branded her brother in the perfect middle of his forehead. I didn't smell burning skin. I didn't see smoke. But in the silence, I saw Preston's mouth form the same circle-shape that was appearing above his eyebrows. Before the quiet broke, I slipped out of the car and ran to my yard, my house.

When I could think again, I understood that Buddy, Preston, and even Sister would never be my best friends. The rules we lived by were different. It was a lonely thought. But I also knew that it was safer not to be part of my neighbors' pack. Outsiders like me could be teased and threatened, but not hit, not burned. I lived in a different country. The line in the grass was not just the Mays' boundary. It also belonged to me.

"Hey," Mama said as I banged through the back door, and then, "What's the matter?"

"Nothing," I told her, because it was too much to tell.

I took my horses to my room and closed the door. My rug was blue water, and I let them drink.

I'll Get
You Back

Jack Barfield was big and mean and poor. We'd known him since second grade, and he'd always been that way. The rest of the class—a combination of polite town kids and brown-armed children who rode the bus to school from their parents' farms in North Carolina's flat tobacco country—had been together since we started school. Being the son of a tenant farmer set Jack apart; his family were neither townsfolk nor landowners. And, too, Jack was a year older than us because Mrs. Sutton had made him repeat second grade. We knew he wasn't stupid, just too mean to learn.

In a way, we depended on Jack to relieve the tedium of our school days. He was always in trouble—for spitting, for throwing rocks, for telling Margie Adams he was going to pick up a damp stick and beat the health out of her, and for arguing with the teacher when Margie told her that he'd said cuss words.

It wasn't all Jack's fault. Common sense said that all red-heads had bad tempers, and Jack's hair was the color of grated carrots. When he was mad, which was most of the time, his face flushed

35

so that his freckles disappeared. We all knew that when you couldn't see Jack's freckles, trouble was about to happen. And for five years now, we'd counted on that trouble to break the monotony of the long, long days at school.

No wonder, then, that we were all pretty excited to see how Jack would get along with Mrs. Cole. Mrs. Cole ("Miz," we said it) had taught seventh grade forever and was every bit as mean as Jack Barfield. But she was teacher-mean, which meant she planned her meanness and used it when it suited her. Unlike Jack, you couldn't tell when Mrs. Cole was mad at you until she was ready to make you pay. She had strategic meanness.

I had heard all this from Preston May. Two years ahead of me in school, Preston usually wouldn't give me the time of day. But he had always regarded it as his delicious duty to prepare me, in gloomiest terms, for what each new year had in store—from the confusion of long division to the sting of the principal's strap. He took particular delight in describing the perils of seventh grade, when I would have Mrs. Cole. "If you talk in class," Preston told me as we sat on the bottom step of his front porch, "she draws a circle on the blackboard and makes you stick your nose in it."

"Well, so did Mrs. Harper, last year," I said. "It wasn't so awful."

"You just don't know," Preston said scornfully. "Mrs. Cole draws that circle high, so you have to get on your toes. And she keeps you there for hours. Sweat and snot get all smeared around in that little chalk ring, and everybody can see it. And in English, if you don't get the first part of your business letter right, she makes you stand in front of the class with a bag on your head."

Preston went on to hint at darker things, but when I asked him for details, he just smiled.

I was determined to stay on Mrs. Cole's good side, so I made up my mind to learn the parts of a business letter the first day of school. Not talking in class would be harder, but I was a town girl with nice town manners, and I believed that would keep me safe. Jack Barfield, on the other hand, had not one manner to his name, and his parents didn't even own the house they lived in. It might be a pretty interesting year.

Of course, we'd seen Mrs. Cole before—eating in the lunch room, doing playground duty during recess. But she looked different facing us that first day—bigger, and though she was smiling, much scarier. She had thin lips and little teeth, like they'd been ground off. Her gray hair was wrapped in a hard ball on the back of her head. She wore a dark blue dress that covered her up from her shoulders to her calves. It had a square neck decorated with little metal studs and a slender belt that buckled around her body in the narrow space between the bottom of her bosom and her waist. We girls noticed because we were beginning to be interested in bosoms. We would learn that she had other dresses, but they varied only in color—dark green, dark maroon, dark gray.

When the clock with the plain round face read 8:00 and the first bell rang, most of the boys, including Jack Barfield, found seats in the back rows. The girls and the three shortest boys sat toward the front. "Children," our teacher said, using a word we believed we'd outgrown, "I'm Mrs. Cole," and we knew. We knew.

And because of that knowledge, seventh grade started out calm. Mrs. Cole's lessons were organized and clear, and in the beginning, no one, not even Jack, tested her famous temper. Among ourselves, we worried that seventh grade could be boring after all.

But by the third week, there were some encouraging developments at recess. A number of the nice girls had joined the Future Homemakers of America with the idea of learning how to remodel our bedrooms. We discussed sewing chintz curtains on our mothers' Singer machines and painting our walls sky blue or butter yellow. Initiation consisted of memorizing and chanting the club's creed—*W-e-e-e are the Future Homemakers of A-mer-ee-ca*—after which each of us received a tee shirt with "FHA" printed on the back and a navy outline of North Carolina on the front. We wore these shirts proudly, believing they identified us as members of a special girls' group. We'd have said "sorority" if we'd known the word. Every evening, we begged our mothers to wash and dry our shirts so they'd be fresh the next day.

One reason we liked the shirts was that they had captured the attention of the boys.

It began as talk. A group of boys would stop playing baseball and form a loose C-shape around a cluster of tee-shirted girls. Pete Sutton, whose daddy owned a lot of tobacco fields, usually started it. "Gosh," he'd say, pointing at a specific spot on a specific tee shirt, "don't you wish you lived right there in Wilson?"

And Jimmy Suggs, the banker's son, would answer, "Oh, I think I'd rather live up in Ashville, right on top of that little hill." The other boys would grin behind their hands, and the girl whose shirt was being scrutinized would blush, pretend to be disgusted, and turn her back, her arms crossed over her chest.

Of course, no nice boy would actually touch a girl's front on the playground, so pointing and grinning was as far as the game went—except one Friday, when it went a little further.

Jack Barfield never took part in the tee-shirt teasing. He wasn't that kind of mean. Or maybe he understood the trouble a tenant farmer's boy could get into if he did something ugly to a respectable girl. But that Friday, Pete decided to get Jack involved.

"Come on over here," he called to Jack, who'd been standing well back from the other boys, his hands in the pockets of his overalls. "C'mere and put your finger on the map, show us where in our great state you'd like to live."

Usually, the other boys were careful not to rile Jack Barfield, partly because working on a farm since he could walk had made him tough and strong, but mostly because when Jack got fighting mad, he drew blood. But the growing excitement of the tee-shirt game had made Pete Sutton careless. When he grabbed Jack by the arm and pushed him closer to the girls, he didn't notice that Jack's face had turned orange-red. "Uh-oh," one of the girls breathed, in anticipation rather than dread. We were far from opposed to violence as entertainment; some of our grandparents had witnessed public hangings. So, a kind of cheer exploded when Jack turned and walloped Pete in the jaw with a hard, freckled fist.

As if summoned by a siren, everyone on the playground came running to see the fight, and a tight, deep ring formed around the boys. Then Mrs. Cole was there. Her "Stop this!" parted the circle and Jack and Pete were exposed, Jack kneeling on Pete's arms and pounding his already bloody nose. Mrs. Cole's practiced hand twisted Jack's ear and brought him to his feet. For one airless moment, we all thought he was going to hit the teacher—a possibility we both feared and hoped for. Such an act would make our class famous forever. We could tell the story to our children. But Mrs. Cole led Jack away, using his ear as a short leash.

As we came in from recess, we saw Jack kneeling again, this time in the hall outside our room. When school ended at 3:15 PM and Mrs. Cole released him with "Jack, you may go," he'd been on his knees for an hour and fifty-five minutes. We understood she'd meant to shame him, to make him look like he was begging. Thus began the cold war between the meanest teacher and the meanest boy in school.

In the weeks that followed, it was clear that Jack was Mrs. Cole's primary target. She made him wear his hand-me-down work shoes on the wrong feet for one whole day when he reversed the "i" and "e" in "chief," and then write the corrected word 100 times on the blackboard during recess. We weren't sure whether she was trying to teach Jack Barfield or break him —like a horse. In fact, we could tell what Jack was learning from our teacher was a mulish obstinance because he'd found a way to get back at her that didn't involve hitting or spitting. When we came in from the playground, he'd just finished misspelling his one-hundredth "cheif."

Even though Mrs. Cole had chosen Jack to pick on, no one— not even the nice kids, not even the nice girls—was exempt from her punishments, a fact I learned first-hand one awful day.

Because of Preston May's warning, I thought I had been vigilant against leaving off the heading of a letter. And yet, here was Mrs. Cole calling me up to the front of the classroom, holding up my neatly but incorrectly written assignment for all to see. "Stand here, Betty," she said, "and you will learn what it feels like not to have a head." She rolled the bottom of a brown paper grocery sack and settled it firmly on my shoulders. I felt the huge weight of disgrace as I fought to breathe inside that sack, and not to cry. For the first time, I knew what it was like to hate a teacher for shaming me. I wish I could say I thought of and sympathized with Jack Barfield kneeling in the hall, but I did not.

And so, when we were not in trouble ourselves, watching the struggle between our mean teacher and our mean classmate grow became our daily entertainment. At recess, the tee-shirt girls discussed whether Jack Barfield was afraid of Mrs. Cole. We decided he was not, but that he might be a little bit afraid of what he would do if she pushed him too hard. In eleventh grade, we would study the Great Themes of Literature: man against man, man against nature, man against god. Now, we had all the drama we could stand watching Jack against Mrs. Cole.

By late fall, we thought we knew all our teacher's tactics—the paper bag punishment, the too-high circle on the blackboard, the exhibition of our worst work on the Wall of Shame. Then one day, she did an amazing thing. Lester Garris had bought a water gun at the dimestore—an orange plastic pistol he'd brought to school even though we all knew the strict rules against firecrackers, chewing gum, or any kind of weapon. He flashed it around before the first bell rang, then hid it in his desk when class began. When he opened his desktop to get out his arithmetic homework,

41

Mrs. Cole was on that gun like a hawk on a rabbit. She held it up with one finger through the trigger guard, as if examining it for prints, then dropped that pistol down the front of her dress into the recesses of her bosom. Silence. Silence. Then our teacher said, "See me after school, Lester." The clock's small hand jumped, and she calmly proceeded to collect the rest of our homework.

At 3:15 PM, the bravest of us, listening outside the door, heard Lester begin to stammer and plead for his pistol. Then fear of discovery triumphed and we all scattered.

When I got home, I saw Preston May hitting a golf ball with a tobacco stick in the yard between our houses. When I said "Hey," he didn't stop hitting, but he said "Hey" back. I walked along beside him until he knocked the ball into a hole he'd dug in the lawn, then asked:

"When you had her, did Mrs. Cole ever take something away from anybody and put it…uh…?"

Preston started to grin. "Wondered when she'd pull that trick. She took my slingshot one time. I brought it home and buried it for three days, like you do when a skunk squirts your clothes."

"Why didn't you tell me before?" I asked.

"Didn't want to spoil the surprise," he said. He fished the golf ball out of the hole, wiped off the dirt on the back of his pants, and went back to hitting.

As the weeks went by, we watched Mrs. Cole and Jack Barfield watch each other. They were being careful, each one circling around the other like the boxers we saw on our snowy TVs. When Mrs. Cole held up a homework paper marked with a red F that filled the whole page and said, "Is anybody brave enough to claim this shoddy work?" Jack answered, "Yes ma'am, I sure am,

Mrs. Cole." We were impressed that he could make polite words sound so hateful—and shocked that Mrs. Cole handed his paper back. If any other boy had sassed her like that, she'd have ripped his paper to pieces and made him tape it back together. Another day, when Jack fell asleep on his desk during reading period, Mrs. Cole walked back and shook his shoulder instead of making the rest of the class stare at him before she clapped her hands next to his ear and called his name. But nobody thought they'd made a truce. Nobody was fooled.

The trouble we'd been waiting for started when the boys were choosing sides for baseball.

"C'mon, Jack," said Jimmy Suggs, "we're short a fielder."

"Nah," said Jack, spitting in the dirt near Jimmy's foot. "It's a dumb game." Although he was strong and a pretty good hitter, his too-big brogans made him clumsy and slow.

"Aw, who needs him anyway," Pete Sutton said. "He runs like his daddy's mule."

"You shut up," Jack said, flushing red and pointing a grimey finger at Pete.

"Oh, I forgot," Pete said to the other boys, failing once more to recognize danger, "Jack's daddy had to sell the mule to buy his boy those fancy shoes."

The laughter stopped when Jack came and stood in front of Pete, leaving only inches between them. For a long minute, the two boys breathed into each other's face. Then, slow and soft, Jack said, "I'll get you back, rich boy." Pete was the one who turned away.

The next day, Jack Barfield had a knife.

He didn't show it to anybody, but we all knew it was a brown and silver pocket knife with the big blade broken off halfway down. One of the girls who rode his bus said she had seen him take it out and polish it with his handkerchief.

During first period the next day, everybody was so quiet the white-faced clock sounded like a mechanical heart. When the bell rang for recess, we filed out to the playground and formed our usual groups, trying not to look at Jack, but knowing exactly where he was. So we were watching when he walked up to the baseball boys and said, "Hey, Pete," and we saw the open knife in his fist.

The other boys shifted backward, so when Pete turned to face Jack, he was standing alone. It was Pete's turn to speak, but he didn't.

The rest of us stood in a circle around them, rigid and silent as fence posts. Then, Mrs. Cole entered the circle, making three at its center.

"Give it to me, Jack," she said, and, after about a hundred heart beats, he closed the knife and gave it to the teacher, though he never took his eyes from Pete. Mrs. Cole held the knife in her palm, then rolled it off her hand down the bosom of her navy-blue dress. Almost gently, she put her hands on Jack's shoulders and turned him to face her.

"I'm sure this knife is valuable to a boy like you," she said, looking down at the bib of the blue denim overalls Jack was wearing. "At the end of the day, you will ask for this knife, as politely as you know how, and then you will never bring this knife to school again. Isn't that right, Jack?"

Jack was looking at our teacher now, looking straight up her nose.

"That could be right, Mrs. Cole," he said, his words steady and low, in a man's voice.

Recess was over. Nothing was settled. The squabble between Jack and Pete was kid stuff. Every one of us knew that the real struggle was between Jack and Mrs. Cole, that what happened at the end of that school day would decide the winner. All of that long afternoon, we sat at our desks, feeling our own hearts ticking to the meaningless words in our dog-eared readers. When the bell rang at 3:15 PM, nobody moved.

"Such good students," Mrs. Cole told us from her station at the side of her big oak desk. Then she said, "Jack, you may come and get your property." When Jack stood up, his face was pale. When he got to the front of the room, it was a painful, bursting red. Mrs. Cole reached deliberately into the front of her dress, took out the knife, and holding it on her flattened hand, offered it to her opponent.

Jack Barfield looked at the knife with yearning and disgust, then took it from the teacher's palm and opened the broken-off blade. The clock jumped forward. He put the knife down on our teacher's desk and pushed it toward her, handle first like our mothers had taught us.

"No thanks, Mrs. Cole," he said. "I reckon you can keep it." Then he wiped his fingers back and forth, back and forth, on the front of his overalls and walked out of the room.

Mrs. Cole sat without moving. Then she put the open knife in her drawer, folded her hands under her bosom, and smiled.

Celery Fight

"Which color looks the best on me?' Carrie Mae asked, holding up a pale green T-shirt and then a kelly green one under her chin. Carrie Mae had green eyes, and any color green looked good on her. In fact, she looked good in any color at all.

Carrie Mae was the head junior varsity cheerleader at her tiny high school in Lake Landing, North Carolina, and that really tells you all you need to know about her. Except that she was also my first cousin. We'd been born six weeks apart, fourteen years ago, to two sisters in their middle thirties who'd stopped expecting children and were bemused by the one apiece who'd showed up. Though my parents and I lived in Southwood, an hour and a half away, we visited my mother's family often, and Carrie and I had grown up together.

"The dark green," I told her. "It gives you cat's eyes." Then I asked, "You think this is a good idea?"

"What? That blue shirt you're putting on?" *My* eyes were blue, in case anybody noticed. I had inherited them from my father.

"No," I said. "Letting our mothers take us to this thing at Charlie's."

"I don't think it's a matter of letting," Carrie Mae said. "They're bound and determined we'll go. I guess they're reliving their youth or something."

"But it's a gas station," I objected. "And who's going to be there? Just people we see all the time, or people we kind of half know?" In spite of its tiny size, I knew Lake Landing's "society" was made up of distinct groups—landowners, fishermen, shrimpers, oystermen, trappers, and farm laborers, mostly—and sometimes, they just plain didn't get along.

"We don't know who'll be there," Carrie Mae said. "That's the fun of it. And, there's a big room behind the gas station. And Charlie just got a jukebox. C'mon. Relax."

"Relax is not what I do," I told her, which she knew very well. While my petite cousin was "cute" and "bubbly," I was usually referred to as "serious," and "studious." Because I'd also inherited my father's height (at fourteen, I was 5' 6" when, luckily, I stopped growing), I played basketball on my school's six-on-six girls' team, not because I was good, but because I was tall. Loving Carrie Mae (and I did, I did) was not always easy. I reminded myself, again, that I had curly hair. And I could sing.

"If you young'uns aren't ready in two minutes, I'm coming up there to bust you open," Aunt Myra called up the stairs. We rolled our eyes at that familiar and unfrightening threat. My aunt was a thin, funny redhead with a lot of sense and a dash of bitterness—but she was never scary.

Carrie Mae, Aunt Myra, and Uncle Bloss lived in the three-story farmhouse my cousin had been born in. As had her daddy. And his daddy. The house, surrounded by pecan trees and camellia bushes, rested in a corner of 300 acres of the richest, blackest land in the Old North State. Uncle Bloss was a Bonner; Aunt Myra, like my mother, was a Gibbs—both old, respected, land-owning families. That made Carrie Mae the county's answer to gentry.

Not that I was jealous.

Unlike my aunt, my mother had married a "furriner." My father, Wade Hampton Ferguson, of whom I was not—ever—ashamed, came from the western part of the state, where the farms were small and the soil was red clay. Now, he taught agriculture at Southwood High School, and wasn't the heir of any recognizable family. And he did not own land. But Daddy stood six feet tall, had black, wavy hair, and was the man to call if a horse (or a boy) needed discipline. Plus, like me, he was musical. For some reason, most people born in Lake Landing seemed genetically unable to carry a tune.

"C'mon, precious baby girls," my mama called. "We're already in the car." In contrast to her sister, my mother was consistently, unaccountably joyful. Carrie Mae and I sometimes wondered if we'd been switched as babies. We grabbed our purses filled with lipsticks and Juicy Fruit, rolled up our jeans above our ankles, and slid into the hot backseat of my family's green Ford.

On the twelve mile trip to Charlie's on narrow NC 14, we passed fields of regal black-green corn and smaller patches of rabbit-tail cotton. With a scornful snort, Aunt Myra pointed out a long, narrow field that had been planted in frilly celery. "When will those Yankees learn that this black dirt is too rich for their fancy crops? They've tried artichokes and eggplants, and now this stuff." We all shook our heads at the willful ignorance of Northerners.

When we drove into the parking lot, tires crunching on a mixture of oyster shells and bottle caps, Mama said, "You girls are going to dance your socks off." I wasn't stupid. I knew this was one of Mama's plots to make her reserved and cautious daughter have more fun. Aunt Myra suspected that Carrie Mae was having more than enough fun already. She wasn't wrong.

"Now go on in," Mama urged us. "We'll wait right here for ten minutes and if you don't come out, we'll figure you're fine. Call us when you're ready to come home. Charlie will let you use the phone. Want a pack of cigarettes to take in with you? They'll make you look sophisticated."

I shook my head at my mother. Carrie would have taken them.

When we looked back, they had rolled the car windows up, leaving only a crack at the top. It would be stifling in the Ford, but they had to keep the mosquitos out. The smoke from Mama's Kools and Aunt Myra's Pall Malls would be further protection.

Carrie Mae and I stopped at the bottom of the wooden steps to perform our ritual: We grinned at each other to make sure neither of us had lipstick on our teeth. Then we shrugged, walked up the steps, and opened the door. Charlie's smelled like beer and sweat and aftershave—not a bad combination. It sounded like Andy Williams singing "Moon River" on the jukebox. It looked like…well, that was hard to say. The windows had been painted black and nailed shut. Three tired oscillating fans moved the gray, smoky air around. We could make out people sitting in booths and a few couples dancing. Carrie Mae gave me a soft nudge with her elbow and I nodded. Charlie's was better than I'd expected.

Then Ben Mills and Matt Tatum appeared, held out their hands, and we became two more couples swaying on the sticky dance floor—one step to the left, one to the right—as the jukebox played "Misty."

Matt and Ben were "friend-friends" rather than boy friends; we'd known them for ages. Like Carrie Mae, Matt and Ben came from "landed" families—which meant they occasionally helped their fathers plant and harvest corn and cotton, but, with their recently acquired drivers licenses, they also had time to go to the beach at Nags Head, to take their flashy outboards and water skis out on the Pamlico Sound, and to develop a keen instinct about how to locate the best parties. Tonight, the best party was at Charlie's.

When "Misty" was over ("*I get mis-ty...just holding your hand*"), the four of us sat down in the booth where the boys had left their beers. Clearly, no matter what your age, if you had the money, you could buy a beer at Charlie's. Mostly for appearance's sake, Carrie Mae and I drank the Cokes Matt brought us, but we also sipped Budweiser from the boys' bottles. And we looked around to see who else had come to this dark, smoky tavern.

Edward Swindell, whose family farm bordered Carrie Mae's, raised his own Bud and came over to join us. Ann Lewis, a big, rough-looking girl I'd seen occasionally, raised her hand but didn't smile, and turned back to her own friends. I noticed another girl with thick, dark hair, the shortest shorts I'd ever seen, and a white blouse so thin her black bra showed through it. (All three males at our table noticed her, too.) She didn't seem to belong to any particular crowd. A cluster of older boys in worn blue jeans and work shirts leaned on the jukebox, drinking and talking. "Fishermen," Ben said. "They're ok guys, make a fair living catching trout and puppy drum." He waved a vague greeting.

"And trapping muskrats and fixing my daddy's combine when the drum won't bite," Edward added.

"Yeah," Matt said, "but they come to church with fish scales on their hands. I wouldn't want my sister to marry one, even if she is a pain in the...Oh, beg pardon, ladies."

Carrie Mae had seen Mary Lou Marshall and Claire Spencer, two girls on her cheerleading squad, on the other side of the dance floor and she got up to say "Hey." My cousin, like my mother, said "Hey" to everybody. "Come right back," Ben said. "Some of these rowdy guys are just waiting to drag a pretty girl like you out the door."

Purposefully, I thought, Carrie Mae walked by a gathering of shrimpers, who looked like they could be rowdy if called upon, and who gave her appreciative looks. The shrimpers, the elite watermen who spent much of their time on the ocean in their handsome, sturdy boats with names like *Mollie's Sweet Dream* and *The Echo of the Lowlands*, had pushed two tables together, where the empty bottles jingled when the jukebox played a fast song.

I recognized one of them—a boy named Aubrey Long. Carrie Mae had pointed him out once at the drugstore, where we went for five-cent pineapple ices. He had nodded at Carrie Mae. And he had smiled at me. He was tan, strong, easy in his body, and beautiful.

Just as a new record settled on the turntable, the door banged open and a bearded man strode in. He raised his head, sniffed like a hunting dog, and proclaimed, "I smell a dead baby." The boys at our table started to laugh and then looked at Carrie Mae and me apologetically. "That's just old Nathan Dans," Matt told us. "He's no-count, but he's harmless. He says that every time he comes in here."

"Yeah, he's all right," Ben said, "but neither one of you girls ought to dance with him. He's got wandering hands."

I was shocked. And excited. And glad to be at Charlie's.

The jukebox started up again and Edward asked me to dance. That is, he held out his hand and raised his eyebrows. As we walked out on the floor, I was happy to realize he was half a head taller than me.

By Charlie's standards, Edward was a smooth dancer, though he shouldn't have hummed untunefully in my ear. He led me in a kind of two step, navigated a couple of turns, and then, extending his left leg under my right one, ended our dance with a dip. I remembered that Margie Adams, a girl in my history class, claimed that you could get pregnant by dipping. I wondered what would happen if, in about five weeks, I called Edward and told him he was going to be a daddy. Then I swallowed a snort. I was thinking like Aunt Myra.

Edward had a pretty smooth line, too. "Um, soft," he said, giving me a little bonus hug. "Is it that pretty blue shirt or the girl inside it?"

"Oh, it's the girl," I assured him, and thought my mother would be proud of me.

I didn't much like Edward, though. He seemed too cocky, too practiced. I glanced over at the shrimpers' table and saw Aubrey Long leaning comfortably against the wall, one leg braced behind him, letting his beer bottle dangle at his side. Edward suffered by comparison. I wondered if Aubrey had seen me, if he remembered me at all.

Several boys had dropped by our table to talk about cars and football, and, I was pretty sure, to see if they could get a dance with Carrie Mae. But Ben, Matt, and Edward had established themselves as our partners and had seated us on the inside of the booth so it was hard to get out. I wasn't sure if they were protecting us or claiming us as their exclusive property. When I saw Aubrey push away from the wall and start in our direction, my deepest hope was that he was coming, not for my pretty cousin, but for me.

Then the door banged open again and three men in their early twenties charged through, carrying a wooden crate of what looked, in the dimness, like bouquets.

"Lord God," said Matt. "It's Shorty Swindell and the Swanquarter crew."

"Fresh from the celery fields," Edward added. "Now we'll have a real party—or a war."

And sure enough, the crate was full of thick stalks of celery, which was being harvested by local men who had no particular job or skill. Except when they found another use for the crop.

"Celery fight!" the man who was obviously Shorty yelled, and he and his cronies slashed the space in front of them with their vegetable swords. Most of Charlie's clientele moved toward the peripheries. Either out of concern for Carrie Mae and me or for themselves, our protectors, laughing a little nervously, packed the five of us into our booth.

Though I was mashed into a corner, I managed to squirm around so I could see. Because I *was* going to watch whatever was about to happen.

What I saw first was how the people in that room divided into new groups—the onlookers and the warriors. What I saw on the faces of the warriors as they moved toward Shorty's challenge was delight. Celery fight! Clearly, there had been others. The prestige among these groups had simply to do with who would win. Some of the fishermen buddied up with Shorty's gang; some joined the shrimpers. Nathan Dans stood on a table, stomping and yelling, "Fight, Goddamn it, fight."

Eagerly, Shorty reached into his crate and tossed weapons to his opponents. Aubrey, at the head of the shrimpers, caught a stalk, broke it apart, and stepped forward, a stiff whip in either hand. Two others followed, flexing proud muscles that came from pulling in heavy, shrimp-laden nets. And the battle began.

I had been pretty sure the whole thing was some kind of joke, a pantomime. I was wrong. The men aimed for faces, bare arms, tender spots below the waist. The girl in the black bra screamed with excitement. There were welts and grunts. There was blood. "Come on, Shorty," Edward shouted.

And Ben said, "Shut up, you idiot. You want that crowd over here, beating on us?"

It was over very quickly. The celery ribs hung limply from the men's hands. Cuts and bruises were examined, exclaimed over. The recent enemies laughed together and bumped each other's shoulders with the sides of their fists. Led by Shorty, his gang began to pick up discarded celery and toss it in the box. Shrimpers and fishermen followed suit.

"Draw?" Shorty suggested.

And Aubrey Long, answering for the shrimpers, said, "Well, ok. Draw. Now, how 'bout if we take on those tough fellas hiding in the corner?"

"Naah." Shorty said. "Them fellas is gentlemen. You know gentlemen ain't gonna fight the likes of us." There was much laughter, and a new round of beer appeared (seemingly by magic; we never saw Charlie).

When someone dropped a quarter in the jukebox, Andy Williams began to sing "Moon River" again.

Then Aubrey was walking purposefully over to our table. I saw Ben and Edward exchange looks and, with some reluctance, get to their feet. We were all sure Aubrey had heard Edward cheering for Shorty. But Aubrey was holding out his hand, palm up. And my cousin—of course he'd come for Carrie Mae—slid out of the booth and they danced to what was left of the song. After the last note (no dip), he walked her back to our table, and re-joined his mates. They up-ended their bottles for the last drops and, slapping shoulders and swapping friendly insults as they went, started for the door. They'd be in their boats before sunrise.

As I believe I mentioned earlier, I wasn't stupid. Yes, my cousin was probably the prettiest girl in that smoky room. But she was also the fourth generation of the wealthiest land-owning family in the county. Aubrey was crossing lines, making a point. On the way out, he nodded meaningfully at non-combatants Ben, Matt, and Edward.

But then he stopped, waved the others on, walked back to our table, and held out his hand to me. To me. A new song had just begun, and we danced, without speaking. When the record ended, he smiled and was gone.

Then the lights blinked three times, Charlie's signal that the night was over. "We'll take you home," Ben offered, but Carrie Mae said, "You know my mama would bust us all open," and went to find the phone—and, I was sure, to see if anything exciting was going on in the gas station part of the tavern. After that, we waited on the steps, swatting late mosquitoes and taking drags off the boys' Marlboros, until the green Ford appeared.

Carrie Mae and I were fourteen, so we were mean enough to make our mothers ask us if we'd had a good time. "You didn't do any damage or cause any trouble, did you?" Aunt Myra demanded of her daughter.

"Oh, no," Carrie Mae answered. "A lot of our friends were there, and we just danced with the boys we knew." My clever cousin was making sure we got to come back to Charlie's.

Mama caught my eye in the rear view mirror. "How about you?" she said.

"It was all right," I said. "I had a pretty good time."

Because I loved my happy mother, I silently promised her that, later on, I'd tell her about the beer and the girl with the see-through blouse and the celery fight. I wouldn't tell her, though, that if Aubrey Long had asked me to, I would have taken off my soft blue shirt and walked out of Charlie's in my white cotton bra to live with him forever on his shrimp boat. It might have worried her. Or maybe it would have made her glad.

Hometown Boy

Mother had promised that on my seventh birthday, I could go downtown by myself. Walking out our front door that afternoon in my brand-new red sandals, I felt very grown-up, very brave. I could see Daddy pretending not to watch me while he trimmed the roses in our backyard, but as he and Mama both knew, I was unlikely to encounter any kind of danger. My journey would cover all of five blocks. And in our little town, everybody knew me, because everybody knew everybody. From the time that I left home to the time I reached Adams' Drug store, where the warm dime in my pocket would buy me a cone of chocolate ice cream, I would be watched, protected—and evaluated.

I waved at Miss Helen Rouse, who made the best lemon meringue pies in town. I grinned at my always-neighbor, some-times-friend Carol Ann (better known as 'Sister'), who was sitting, almost hidden, on a low branch of her magnolia tree. And I summoned the courage to nod at gruff old Mr. Fields, wearing his bow tie and rocking in his squeaky chair, as usual, on his once-elegant front porch.

At the drugstore, Mr. Adams himself gave me an extra scoop of ice cream and wished me happy birthday. By the time I got home, mouth and hands sticky with chocolate, Mr. Fields had called my mother. "He wasn't mean," she assured me. "He just thinks you should hold your shoulders up and not be so shy." My mother had more than once given me this very advice, but Mr. Fields spoke with the voice of the community, and even then, I knew I would be wise to heed it. That voice also spoke to Vic Garris, who had the nerve to ignore it and was punished for his courage.

By the time I turned seven, I'd been friends with Vic for one year, since we both had had Mrs. Thompson for our first-grade teacher. We were two of four students in the Red Bird reading group, so I knew that Vic, unlike most other boys, didn't hate books. I also knew that, unlike *all* other boys, Vic *did* hate football. Later, he told me that he'd hated it ever since his father took time off from painting houses to watch him play in a neighborhood game of "flag." "You got to try, son!"he yelled. "At least try!"

Try what? young Vic wondered. Try to grab the dirty red bandana out of Ralph Altman's back pocket? Try to trip his friend Glenn Scott, who was the same age as Vic, but half his size?

"Damn," his father muttered, sticking his hands deep in the pockets of his paint-splattered overalls and shaking his head slowly. "Damn."

That night at supper, Vic's mother, a dark-haired woman whose skin on her right jaw had been melted long-ago in a kitchen fire, tried to soothe her husband: "Ed, he's a good boy, and he likes to do a lot of other things. He fixed the lawnmower and he helped Kenny with his spelling."

"But he's got potential for the game, Lois," his father said. "He's smart and he's big—and football might get him out of this little bitty, stuck-up town and into college."

She patted her husband's arm. "Well, it's the little bitty town where you grew up," she teased, "and you want bragging rights while he's here."

They talked as if he'd left the table, but Vic knew his father was speaking to him. His little brother Kenny happily shook more catsup onto his meatloaf. It was already clear that Kenny would be neither big nor smart, and Vic pitied, loved, and envied him.

By the time Vic and I were in fifth grade, Ed Garris had pretty much given up on ever seeing his first-born in helmet and pads. When the men downtown said, "In a couple of years, that big old boy of yours will make a fine halfback. He is gonna try out, right?" Ed pulled his once-white cap down a notch and shrugged. "'Course he will, 'course he will," said Roger Wooten, pleasantly. "His daddy played, didn't you, Ed—not that you were ever real good. And you didn't raise that boy soft or lazy—or yellow." Glances were exchanged, and then somebody mentioned Raymond Frye's new Ford pickup and the talk moved on.

Vic wasn't lazy. He'd been working at Manzelli's grocery since he turned ten. He wasn't soft—every week, he stacked cans of tuna and Campbell soup along the walls of the storeroom. And he wasn't yellow—he'd tear the arms off anybody who picked on Kenny. He just didn't like football.

The town library was in what had been the two parlors of Miss Burke's many-windowed house. Miss Burke was, by default, the librarian. Vic had first gone there to search for car repair manuals—he'd graduated from the lawn mower to his father's dented truck, which had a chronic cough. He kept going back to the library because Miss Burke made sugar cookies for young patrons on Tuesday afternoons. After awhile, she began to add books to Vic's stack of magazines: *The Three Musketeers*, *Huckleberry Finn*, and, later, *A Farewell to Arms*, books she'd already sent home with me. By then, my love of reading had earned me an undeserved reputation as a scholar. Few people knew how pitiful I was at math and science.

Soon, Vic and I discovered we liked the same books—partly because the selection was limited, and partly because otherwise gentle Miss Burke had definite ideas about what young people should and should not read. Vic and I would sit on the library's front steps (one did not talk in the library) and wonder if mosquitoes bothered Huck and Jim and if Frederick Henry left the army because he was a coward or because he was brave. Our rambling talk drew us together, and by eighth grade, we were regarded as a couple. Our classmates teased us sometimes.

"What do you two lovebirds talk about?" George Altman asked suspiciously. "Algebra?"

I smiled, knowing that Vic could keep up his end of such a conversation, but I'd have little to say. But the teasing from our school friends was not the same as the teasing that began for Vic in the summer before we entered high school. It started at Manzelli's grocery and it had nothing to do with algebra or me. It had everything to do with Vic and football.

Vic had always liked working at the grocery with its green and white awning. Mr. Manzelli was a soft-spoken man whose white apron splotched with red and brown reminded Vic of his father's overalls. And Vic liked the friendly businessmen who stopped in to pick up a pack of Camels and often included him in their banter: "I expect Gerald keeps you around to read the hard words on the soup cans, right, young Vic?" Mr. Wooten might say. Like Ed Garris, Gerald Manzelli worked hard, keeping his store open early to late. He had to, he told Vic, to keep his customers away from the big Winn-Dixie twenty miles down the road—and to keep the town's citizens from remembering that "Manzelli" was a "Spick" name, strange and foreign among the Wootens and Suttons and Wrights. "These are good people, boy, but it don't do to be different in this little town. Better for business to be one of the folks."

And so, it didn't surprise Vic much when Mr. Manzelli began saying, "When does practice start, boy? You know we can change your schedule to suit Coach Randall." Vic had explained to the grocer that football didn't make sense to him, that he would not try out for the freshman team, would not be going to practice, but the man hadn't believed him. "Tell Coach you got those muscles working here, boy. Maybe I'll get the whole team unloading canned corn and pork and beans."

Gradually, the easy, meaningless exchange that Vic had always enjoyed with the customers reshaped itself into something more intense, less friendly. "Hey boy," Mayor Stub May would say, "gonna be putting that brainy head inside a blue and white helmet next month, aren't you? Got to pay your dues, you know."

Even at home, Vic told me, he couldn't get away from football. His mother encouraged him to stick to his decision. She'd be so glad not to have to worry about him getting hurt or hurting someone else. But she, too, had been getting questions at church and from neighbors that she didn't know how to answer. And Kenny—gentle, laughing Kenny—told him he'd punched a kid at school for saying that anybody who didn't play football was a pussy.

His father, Vic said, was worst of all because he was trying so hard to be on his son's side—and doing such a rotten job of it.

The library, as always, was a refuge, and we'd meet there when Vic got off work in the late afternoons. Miss Burke, bless her heart, had never heard of football, or if she had, she refused to acknowledge it, and she'd found a corner for us where we could read and whisper "as long as you don't disturb the other patrons"—of which there were few, or none. And so, we sat in our private space that smelled like sugar cookies and slightly mildewed books, and Vic felt safe, for a while. One day, in the near-whisper Miss Burke allowed us, Vic said, "I don't like it that in all these stories, something big has to change. Huck and Jim get on the raft, and in *The Grapes of Wrath*, the Judds go to California. There's a lot of upheaval, a lot of leaving, and it's all sad."

"Yeah," I said, "not like here where Mr. Fields always wears a bow tie and the drug store always has vanilla, chocolate, and strawberry ice cream. And people live in the same house all their lives."

"Like our folks," Vic said. "Like we will."

Would we? I wondered. *Would I?*

Much of that summer was slow and easy and simple. The smell of fresh-cut grass added weight and sweetness to the air. Vic worked most days, but the town had relaxed into warm-weather pace. Mr. Manzelli's customers were happy to lounge and chat about tomatoes or fishing for blue gill at the river. It was too hot to think about football. In the long, late afternoons, Vic and his neighbor Glenn Scott, the second smartest boy in our class, tinkered behind Glenn's house on an old green and cream Chevy they'd soon be old enough to drive.

Glenn's girlfriend Carolyn and I sat in folding lawn chairs, tanning our legs and drinking Cokes with peanuts we dropped in the bottles. Some evenings, a few kids a year ahead of us would organize a trip to the drive-in movie, and we smuggled in an extra or two in the trunks of their cars. We felt very daring, though Mrs. Rose, who owned the Twilight Drive-In and knew all our parents, was completely aware of our mischief.

Then, on August 14th, two weeks before the first day of school, football practice began, and Vic realized he'd been granted a stay of execution, not a pardon.

He knew first from Mr. Manzelli. Vic noticed his subdued greeting that Monday morning, and the troubled stoop of the grocer's shoulders. "Sit down, Vic, I got something hard to say. Folks are asking questions. They want to know if something's wrong with you. They think maybe you got no guts. They say I shouldn't have no chicken working for me. Then they laugh, like they made a big joke. Now, I know you're not scared. I like you, boy, you know I do. But you're gettin' bad for business. You can finish out the week, but I'm not going to be able to keep you on."

In the next few days, Vic realized that people got quiet when he walked down the street, that they turned slightly away—no nods, no two-fingered waves. When he stopped in the drugstore to pick up some aspirin for his mother, Mr. Adams made him wait ten minutes before acknowledging his presence, then took his money and slapped the bottle on the table without a word. At home, when Kenny asked innocently if they could throw the football in their shady backyard, Vic laughed, then went to the room he shared with his brother and softly closed the door.

The library was stifling in August, so he and I met in the town's little park, where two old oaks shaded the netless tennis court, and sat in the swings, whose heavy chains were hot in our hands. Vic caught me up on most of what was happening. I guessed he was protecting me from the ugliest parts. He kept wanting to change the subject.

"Let's discuss movies," he said, "or popcorn."

"Or algebra," I said, and we laughed, sort of.

But other kids were eager to tell me the darker stories—how someone had tied white handkerchiefs to the Garris' mailbox, how someone (someone with talent, so it had to be Carl Creech, who was also captain of the football team) had painted pansies on the hood of the old Chevy in Glenn's backyard. It was Carolyn who told me about the car. "I used to wish Glenn was as big and strong as Vic," she said, "but now I'm glad he's a little scrawny thing. Nobody wants him on any sports team."

And then she asked me, "Are you going to break up with him?"

"No," I said. "It never crossed my mind," which wasn't absolutely true. I'd begun to feel the collateral damage of Vic's

64

decision. "How's it feel to be dating a fag?" was the worst so far. And I'm not proud to admit that I sometimes imagined how much fun I would have had as the girlfriend of a football star. But, no, I was Vic's friend as well as his girl, and I'd be loyal, for as long as I could.

When school started, Vic's situation got worse. The kids were irritating, but their comments usually took the form of clumsy teasing. The teachers were more direct, and completely serious. Mr. Grant, the high school principal, was an erect, stern man, a former Marine. That first day of school, he told Vic to stay after class. Waiting in the hall for Vic to be released, I overheard some of what Mr. Grant had to say. "Talented...talented academically and, I'm sure, athletically...should put your school and your community above your own preferences...may be acting selfishly. And four years of football...high school record...recommendations from teachers...something to think about. You can go now. I see your girlfriend's waiting."

"I think I've been complimented, lectured, and threatened, all in less than five minutes. He's good," Vic said when we were, we hoped, out of earshot.

Mrs. Walker was tougher. We liked her. All the "smart" kids did. She was short, with cotton candy hair and a round face, but she was fierce, and passionate about English literature, particularly Shakespeare. Vic told me, almost word for word I expect, what she kept him after school to tell him:

"Do you know what shunning is? Have you read about that practice? It's what happens when a family or community shuts out one of its members. They will not speak to him, look at him, or acknowledge his presence. It's worse, I think, than Romeo's banishment because it's carried out by people who once loved him. And that's what's happening to you, Vic Garris.

"We're talking about two kinds of games here, you know. One is simple, brutal, and stupid, but it has rules and boundaries and you only have to play on weekends. The other is vague, complex, and all-inclusive, and everyone you know is playing all the time. The rules change, your teammates change. It's called—sorry to be obvious—life. You may decide you have to play the simple game in order to play the big one. There's no dishonor in that decision."

We were sitting in the front seat of the old Chevy. The summer evenings were getting shorter but no cooler. The plastic seat covers stuck to the back of my legs. Periodically, Vic lifted the arm he had around my shoulder to let the air circulate. It was too hot to kiss. Vic scared me when he suddenly pushed back on the steering wheel and then hit it with his fist so hard it shook. Then he looked at me gently. "That's what they do in novels, you know. I wanted to see how it felt. Silly, is how."

Then he said, "I'm going to play. I'm telling you first. I'll tell my folks tonight. Tomorrow, I'll tell Coach Randall. What do you think?"

What I felt was relief—for him, for me. The community would let him back in; people would talk to him again. I imagined myself cheering for Vic as he made yet another tackle, caught yet another pass (and there my knowledge of football ended). I imagined being envied by the other girls. And, with what I knew was terrible unfairness, I blamed Vic for backing down, for caving in. I looked for words. "I know it's hard," I said. "I would have done it a long time ago. Seems to me you had to choose between moving away, cutting off your right arm at the shoulder, or playing football. You made the only possible choice."

"Well, I never considered moving away," he said. "Have you?" And though I didn't answer, he held my hand as we walked the two blocks to my house.

In the next weeks, I saw very little of Vic. He'd call me after practice, exhausted, and we'd talk a few minutes. Mostly, I'd talk.

"How was it?"

"Hard."

"Are the other guys nice to you?"

"Nice is a funny word to use, but yeah, nice enough, most of them."

"Is Coach Randall nice to you?"

"No. But he's an s.o.b.—sorry—to everybody, so it doesn't matter."

"Are you ok?"

"Sure."

One blue and breezy Sunday, we walked to the park. I watched him settle himself gingerly on the hard seat of the swing.

"Sore?" I asked.

"Let me count the ways."

"Tell me what your folks said when you told them you were going to play."

"Mom cried. I don't know if she was relieved or scared or disappointed. But it didn't last long. She said, 'I expect it's for the best, Vic.' Kenny hugged me around the waist. Dad patted my shoulder, then shook his head, just like he did when I told him I wasn't going to play."

"Tell me about the other people—if you feel like it."

"Well, Coach Randall said, 'About God-damned time, Garris'—sorry. Coaches have the corner on cursing. Mr. Manzelli said, 'Good, good. Your job's waiting when the season's over.' Folks downtown just pretend nothing happened."

"Are you ok, Vic?" I asked.

"Yep," he said as he hauled himself out of the swing. "Now that I'm not a leper anymore, let's go to the drugstore and talk about great big chocolate ice cream cones."

At the beginning of that season, I knew only this about football: the goal was the goal, the boys wore so much equipment that you couldn't tell who was who, the opposing teams lined up facing each other and tried to hurt anybody with a different colored shirt on. Like Vic, I couldn't see much sense in it, though I lacked the courage to say so. But I liked the cool evenings and the smell of leaf smoke and our not-very-good marching band. And I really liked hearing people cheer for Vic, as I had known I would.

When the season ended, I hadn't learned much more about the game and the opposing teams. Vic didn't offer much information. Once, when I asked, he tried to explain a play, but the diagram he drew reminded me of math class and my brain shut off. Once, I asked him what the players said to each other when they were all piled up on the field. "You don't want to know," he said.

"Do you say that stuff?"

He hesitated, then said, "I'm quoting Mrs. Walker quoting Macbeth. 'Be innocent of the knowledge, dearest Chuck.'" And we laughed about a man calling his wife "Chuck."

Ed Garris had been right—Vic was good. By junior year, he was starting every game, and as a senior, he was co-captain and All-Conference. At the homecoming game that October, I watched with pleasure as he pulled passes out of the air and dodged tackles. By half-time, he'd scored two touchdowns.

It was one of those perfect fall nights—chilly enough for jackets, almost bright enough to play by moonlight. I loved the excitement, the colors, loved being the hero's girlfriend. From where I sat in the bleachers with Glenn and Carolyn and a gaggle of classmates, I could see Vic's parents positioned right on the 50-yard line, stiff with pride and nerves. Kenny, I knew, was somewhere in the crowd, smiling, about to burst with happiness.

When I got up to get a Coke, many hands reached up to help me navigate the noisy metal steps. At the refreshment stand, I heard a group of men discussing the game. The mayor was talking while Mr. Adams and Mr. Wooten listened. I moved closer to them, certain they'd be praising Vic. And they were. "He's good, maybe the best we've had. He's gonna win us the championship this year."

"You know we made that boy." This from Mr. Wooten.

"'Course we did," agreed a man who worked at the hardware store.

"Without us, he'd never have found the gumption to play. God knows, his daddy was no help. Didn't have the sense to push that boy."

"Yeah, well, Ed never was much count. Didn't have two dimes or two brains to rub together," said Mr. Adams.

"Or two balls, either," added another man, and the others snorted in appreciation, put their caps or fists to their mouth, and laughed.

"Team won't be much next year without Vic. But, hey, hasn't he got a younger brother—Donny or Johnny?"

"Kenny. It's Kenny. But nah, he's a soft brain. Not worth our trouble."

I stood there. The shunning had been bad, the taunts of other students and pressure from teachers hurtful. But I had just heard the town's most respected men speak with the voice of the community, and what they said was hateful. I made myself move, carried my watery Coke back to the bleachers. *This is the town that Vic loves*, I thought. And then, *Do I tell Vic? Do I tell him?*

The team was just coming back on the field. I spotted Vic, wearing number 42. I watched him bring the other players into the huddle, saw them put their hands together in the middle of the circle, and I heard their joyful "Go, Rams!" And I knew I wouldn't—couldn't—tell Vic what I'd heard.

After Christmas, Vic began to get recruiting letters and calls promising a variety of scholarships and financial aid. But he turned down these glittering opportunities for a modestly good academic scholarship to a modestly good school about an hour's drive from home.

I applied to one college as far away as I could get and still pay in-state tuition. I knew that, though I loved my parents and many things about the town where I had grown up, I would not live there again. Vic and I saw each other on occasional weekends, and at first it was a deep, comfortable relief to be together. But gradually, we had less and less to talk about, and after a while, we just didn't see each other anymore.

I took a job teaching high school English in the western part of the state. I went home on holidays. After Vic graduated from law school, he opened an office on Main Street two doors down from Manzelli's grocery. I heard that he had married a gentle, smiling girl who'd been two years behind us in school.

I wonder if they go to football games.

Just The Way
It Was

James L. Howard owned the funeral home in our single-stoplight town of Southwood, North Carolina, and he looked a little bit like Humphrey Bogart. It was a resemblance he cultivated—low, sexy voice; hair slicked back, no part. James L. (my parents knew him well, so I didn't have to call him "Mr."; he called me "Kiddo") had married an elegant, dark-haired woman named Camille Gilliam, of *the* Gilliams, an old East Coast family. James L. drove a powder-blue Cadillac, and the Howards had the town's only backyard swimming pool.

In spite of—or because of—all these things, everybody liked James L. and Camille. James L.'s father, Mr. Howard, had been a great benefactor to little Southwood. In fact, he was so revered that no one ever said his first name. For all I knew, he didn't have one. After making a success of the Howard Funeral Home, he paid for the merry-go-round, swings, and slide in the town's only park, commissioned the big stained-glass window of Jesus the Shepherd at the Methodist church, and planted crepe myrtles along both sides of Main Street. He and his wife had three sons—Lindsay, Raymond, and James L. He died believing that the Howard business and name were guaranteed for at least several generations.

But Raymond was an alcoholic and Lindsay was a philanderer—handsome, suave, and, in the eyes of the community, "sorry." He helped at the funeral home sometimes, and people tolerated him, but didn't trust him like they did James L. How, they asked, could you count on anybody who'd been married—and left—three times? That made James L. the family's white sheep, a good businessman and a good citizen, carrying on his father's philanthropy. The Cub Scouts were often invited to swim in the pool—if they showered at home first. When a family couldn't afford a good funeral, they got one anyway. So, the town figured he'd earned his swanky car and swimming pool. And besides, who wanted an undertaker who always behaved like—an undertaker?

Camille taught music at the high school and had written the school's fight song: *Southwood, Southwood, we'll always stand with you.* She also gave private piano lessons at home. I was one of her Friday afternoon students, and, for her sake, I hoped her other pupils had more enthusiasm and talent. She was kind to me—expert, efficient, and always a little reserved. I sometimes wondered if she'd rather be living in a big city, playing in an orchestra or maybe a classy, smoky bar.

The Howards didn't have children. To me, they didn't seem like the children type. In fact, I believe James L. and Camille and my parents became good friends because, for a long time, both couples were childless. When I came along—a surprise to everyone, I suspect—I was more or less absorbed into the friendship. They continued to have their Friday night rummy parties, meeting at one house or the other for bourbon and 7-Up, T-bone steaks, and cards. Like Camille, my father and mother taught at the high school—math and home economics, respectively—and since teachers couldn't be seen drinking alcohol, around the time I was five, I began to stand lookout, answering the door if someone knocked and stalling until the evidence could be hidden. (Of course, in our little town, everybody knew what everybody else wore, spent, ate, and drank, but as long as your sins were subtle and civil, they were ignored or tolerated. And anyway, nobody expected a man who looked like Humphrey Bogart to hang out with teetotalers.)

Not that our town was forgiving of blatant misdeeds it couldn't ignore. My parents often cautioned me: "If you have to misbehave, come home to do it. If Mrs. Cole hears you using bad language at school, if Mr. Hardy at the post office catches you riding your bike on the sidewalks downtown, you'll be in all kinds of trouble. You—and we—have a reputation to maintain. And you know about reputations—they're like...."

"Like teacups," I'd finish. "'Once broken, never mended.' I'll be very, very, very careful." And I was.

I loved going to the Howards' house because Camille never mentioned my sad performance at the piano, and I got to eat with the grown-ups. Camille's wedding silver was the heavy, ornate kind, and the knife handles always shone. After dessert (my favorite part) I could read myself to sleep in the big four-poster guest bed, listening to the laughter and talk from the rummy table and feeling completely, deeply safe. Sometimes, Camille would let me look through her jewelry box, and for my tenth birthday, she let me choose a ring from her collection. After much consideration, I chose a gold ring with a small emerald stone—which I lost before I'd even turned eleven. Camille never mentioned it.

The ritual dinner and rummy parties might have gone on until somebody began to forget the rules, but not long after I lost the ring, a new couple came to town. James Spencer, the town's new doctor, and his beautiful wife Diane, who had been his nurse before the two little boys came along, moved into a handsome old house shaded by hundred-year-old oak trees. Oh, people gossiped at first—that's how a small town entertains itself. Diane, rumor said, was Dr. James's second wife. With her long blonde hair and ready laugh, she might have lured him out of his first marriage. And maybe Diane had been married before; the doctor might or might not be the father of the two boys—active, fair-haired fellows of four and six. To me, this was adult business, uncomfortable stuff I'd rather not know.

But little by little, the family became a familiar part of the town and people stopped wondering about their history. After all, no one even noticed that the grocer was named Pink Moose (really) or that Miss Junie, the school lunch lady, wore her dresses wrong side out.

"That's just the way it is," we said, a formula that soon applied to the Spencers.

Besides, James Spencer (who became Doc J.) was a good doctor. He was tall, thin, and sometimes a little socially awkward, but he was willing to make house calls, glad to talk about a mole or sore back at the grocery store or post office. And no one could resist Diane, who liked to play bridge (but had the good sense

75

to lose often), wore such pretty clothes, and volunteered for everything. The family was invited to backyard barbeques, football games at the high school, and, eventually, to steak-and-rummy Friday nights.

And the long-established, cozy, predictable atmosphere of those evenings shifted a bit. The well-behaved boys, Michael and David, came for the first half hour or so, to paddle in the pool and eat ice cream. Then they went home to the babysitter (a job for which I never volunteered). After that, the drinks got just a little stronger, the jokes a little more suggestive. The rummy games gave way to poker and the stakes got a little higher (a quarter rather than a nickel a hand). I didn't mind. In fact, I liked the change. I related the jokes—even the ones I didn't understand—to my girlfriends at school, and they giggled, even if they didn't understand either.

While the grown-ups were sipping their bourbon and 7-Up, I was moving close to my first teen-age year, and one night Doc J. handed me a drink he'd made especially for me. It was pale amber and had four maraschino cherries at the bottom. "Doctor's orders," he said. "It's time for you to know how whiskey makes you feel. Pretty soon, you're going to have to say "no" to some naughty boy who's trying to get you tipsy."

James L. chuckled and said, "Drink up, Kiddo." When I looked to my father for permission, he nodded and said, "Just sip slow, Betty." And I sat among them proudly, dipping shrimp into cocktail sauce and nursing my first glass of sophistication.

Soon, Mother and Camille invited Diane to join the Lyceum Book Club. The other members were delighted, since when it was Diane's time to entertain, they had a chance to admire how she had decorated the Spencers' big house. All the ladies just loved the living room wallpaper with its big yellow roses. And everyone—with the possible exception of Mrs. Creech, the Methodist preacher's wife—appreciated *Tobacco Road*, which Diane recommended as a "classic" for the April book. I benefited as well. Several nights of reading my mother's copy significantly broadened my knowledge of sex.

And Diane treated me in a way that Camille, with her natural reserve, could not. Energetic and playful, the doctor's wife seemed not much older than me. Once, when she invited me over to help entertain Michael and David, she told me that she thought "Kay and Charles" were "darling," a term I'd never associated with my parents. She went on: "To tell the truth, when we first met them, I thought, 'They're school teachers—probably kind of dull,' but they're really cute and funny." Then, Diane loaned me her little velvet cape with ermine tails to wear to my first spring prom, putting it in a nice store bag for protection and assuring me that she wanted to come over and see me when I was all dressed up.

Walking home, I reached into the bag to touch the fur and velvet, and imagined that wearing the elegant wrap would make me look more like its glamorous owner. I also tried, unsuccessfully, to imagine my parents as "cute," though I was a little confused that Diane had thought they might not be fun because they taught school. It was easier, I decided, when grown-ups didn't tell me what they thought.

By now, we all knew that Diane was a giver—sunflower seeds for the Audubon Club, a rosebush for my mother, opera tickets in Raleigh for Camille, milk in a bowl for the stray cat. She'd asked to be included in the Meals on Wheels route that Mother and Camille had done for years, and they said the deliveries took twice as long because Diane included a little present—a Hershey's kiss, a tiny nail file—with everyone's dinner and always wanted to stay and chat.

"Well," they said, "that's just the way Diane is."

"I sometimes suspect that James L. is sad that he and Camille didn't have children." This was my mother telling me more adult stuff I didn't want to know. I liked to think that grown-ups were immune to regrets and disappointments, just as they never seemed to catch mumps or chicken pox. She had taken me to Siler City to buy some loafers I'd been yearning for, and we were having our usual raisin bread sandwiches with cream cheese and olives at the Woolworth's counter. "Have you noticed how he loves the Spencer boys?" my mother asked.

I *had* noticed, and sometimes felt a little jealous of James L.'s friendliness toward David and Michael. He'd always been nice to me, but kept his distance. Now he bought the boys blow-up toys to play with in the pool and took them riding in the Cadillac with all the windows down. Then, Mother said, "Camille has a tipped uterus and couldn't get pregnant"—which was *way* more than I wanted to know.

On the evening of the dance, both Diane and Camille came by to see me in my finery and tease me a little about my date (I was going with Preston May from next door, an arrangement of convenience rather than passion). I enjoyed their admiration, though I knew it was mostly for my mother's sake. Camille said, "You look lovely, Betty." Diane said, "Oh honey, you are scrumptious with your little high heels and forget-me-not eyes. You'll be the star, the darling of the dance." Two styles—Camille kind and restrained, Diane exuberant and bubbly. Sometime during the night, I lost one of the ermine tails on Diane's cape, and though my mother apologized profusely, Diane never said a word to me about it.

One night when we were all at the Spencers' place for a cookout (Doc J. was a wizard with barbequed chicken and in great demand as a cook for Rotary dinners), Diane asked me to help her pour the inevitable sweet tea in the kitchen. I liked arranging the sweating glasses on her silver tray and listening to the ice cubes crack in the liquid. She leaned on the counter. "I want to tell you a happy secret," she said "I'm going to have a baby."

I thought a baby would be cute and said so. She hugged me and said, "Maybe you'll babysit for all three of the Spencer children sometimes," and laughed at my alarmed expression. "Just teasing, honey," and we carried the drinks out to the patio.

In a few weeks, the whole town knew, and there was much rejoicing and celebration—baby showers, baby blankets, baby booties. About two months before Diane's due date, Camille gave the most elegant party of all, which, untraditionally, included both women and men, and a few select children—Michael and David and me. I thought Camille's silver, her mother's china and crystal, and the vases of yellow roses made the house look like the Biltmore mansion. And it was full-to-bursting of people who had known each other forever. The Spencers were the newest newcomers, and they'd long since ceased to be new. Diane looked beautiful, of course, in a long, floating dress the color of daffodils. She pretended to sulk when her husband wouldn't let her have a glass of champagne. (Champagne wasn't like bourbon. Everybody, even school teachers, could drink champagne in public.)

And soon afterwards, the baby arrived—a perfect, dark-haired little boy. My mother told me it had been a very easy delivery, which was enough information for me.

When Mother and I went to the hospital to visit, James L. was just leaving. He'd brought a bowl of shining fruit for Diane and three presents, one for each of the boys. Diane welcomed us and pushed the blanket away from her new son's face so we could see. I thought he looked like a hairless puppy. Mother said he was precious. "Did you decide on a name?" she asked.

Smiling, Diane said, "James."

From the start, Jimmy (we had too many "Jameses" already) was different from his brothers—darker, smaller. Did people talk? Of course, they did. "Is he all right? You know, 'all there?' Will he be a dwarf or something? Too bad, with the other two so bright and handsome." But Jimmy was "all there," with interest. Soon, everyone acknowledged that he was more athletic, and a little more assertive, than either of his brothers, who sometimes seemed shy. In fact, as Jimmy grew up and became more social, he became a town favorite. "Hey, Mr. Moose. Hey, Miz Burke," he'd greet the grocer and the librarian. "Just like Diane," people said. "So friendly. Not a shy bone in his body." In Southwood, all doors opened to Jimmy Spencer.

But of all places in town, Jimmy preferred the Howards' pool. Even in March and October, when the water was too cold for his brothers (and certainly for me), he begged to go swimming. James L. and Camille's pool became a gathering place for the now much-expanded Friday night steak/rummy/poker/bourbon/

swimming group. On thick summer evenings, when the lawns had been burned crisp and brown and the trees were tired of their leaves, I enjoyed sitting on the edge of the pool, my feet in the water, watching the three boys. Michael took his role as older brother seriously. "Don't run, you guys," he'd say. "It's slick," and "Come on out and eat now. Hamburgers are ready." David and Jimmy squabbled sometimes. It was hard for the middle child that the baby was a better swimmer. But usually, the three coexisted happily.

As for me, I liked being an observer. From my pool position, halfway between the boys and the adults, I could splash with the kids, chat with the grown-ups, or just watch, my eyes half closed against the sun. One of the things I saw was how much James L. loved Jimmy. *Well*, I thought, *everybody loves Jimmy.* And Jimmy, as most children do, responded to this attention.

At all our gatherings, he followed "Uncle L." around, picking up on some of his mannerisms. We all laughed at the little boy's pretty good imitation of James L.'s gangster swagger, which was straight out of *Casablanca*.

The summer Jimmy was four, James L. added a sixteen foot speedboat to what Camille called his "toys." "It certainly wasn't my idea," I heard her say to Diane and my mother. "I'm like a cat—can't stand to get wet." But the rest of us appreciated the sleek, powerful machine. David and Michael learned to water ski at nearby White Lake—and so did I, but the boys were more daring and soon were crossing the wake and skiing backwards, making their parents nervous and proud. When Jimmy pouted because he was too little to ski, James L. took him in his lap and let him steer the boat. Soon, we were calling the boy "Skipper," and I heard James L. say to Jimmy, "I'm glad you like the ship, Kiddo. When I die it will be yours."

And when Jimmy replied eagerly, "Oh, are you going to die soon?" James L. laughed. That night, at supper, he repeated the conversation as proof Jimmy was "one smart young-un." With the possible exception of Camille, we were all sorry when the weather got chilly—by Southwood's standards—and the boat was stored in the marina for the short winter.

One day that fall, I came home from basketball practice to hear my mother and Camille talking in the living room. Their serious tones kept me from going right in to say hello, and I heard Mother say, "Does it make you sad?" I'd never thought of Camille as being anything but Camille—strong, steady, in control. And I was relieved when she said, "No, I'm not really sad—or jealous. James L. doesn't give me any reason to be." I imagined then what they were discussing so intently: Mother must be worried that Camille felt bad about not having children, and thought that James L.'s affection for the Spencer boys, especially Jimmy, was hurting her feelings. Satisfied with my insight, and anxious not to have them think I was eavesdropping, I dropped my books emphatically on the kitchen table and called out "Hey, you two" before I joined them, putting a stop to their intimacies.

In bed that night, I started to acknowledge another reason that Camille might be sad or jealous, but I pushed it right out of my head and went to sleep.

Preston May had turned out to be a pretty good quarterback, and the night before Homecoming, our neighbors threw a big cookout in their backyard. This year, excitement was high be-cause the Rams were tied for first place in the conference with our long-time rivals, Goldston. The night was perfect—crisp and clear. The men were basting chicken, flipping hamburgers, and grilling hot dogs for the kids. Women in jackets and scarves brought potato salad, coleslaw, pecan pies, and coconut cakes. Nobody drank bourbon, of course, but men could pull beers from ice chests, and youngsters drank Cokes and Pepsis and 7-Ups. Most of the women sipped sweet tea.

The Howards and Spencers were there. Diane, her blonde hair in a shiny French twist, visited with everybody. The boys tossed a football, shouting, "Hike!" and "First down!" Jimmy did a pretty impressive imitation of James L. imitating Humphrey Bogart. The night was especially exciting to me because my cousin Carrie from down East was spending the weekend with me, and we'd be meeting two very cool boys at the game later on. Carrie reminded me of Diane in some ways—very social, never shy. When everybody had filled a paper plate, found a place to sit, and started to enjoy the bounty, Carrie said in her cheerleader voice, "That little Jimmy looks just like James L. Howard."

Everything stopped. Plastic forks were suspended, conversation died. Only the boys' football game went on, unaffected. And then, as if someone had said "Go," everything started again. Carrie whispered, "What just happened?"

And I said, "Oh, nothing. Let's go get some of Mrs. Hardy's pound cake before it's gone."

On Sunday night when the excitement from Homecoming was over (we won), and Carrie's parents had come to take her home (we'd had a great time at the victory dance), I went to find my mother. She was sitting at her dresser, rubbing Pond's

Cold Cream on her cheeks. I sat on the bed. This time, I wanted information.

"Mother," I said, "is James L. Jimmy's father?"

"Yes, Betty, he is," she answered.

"And has everybody known it for a long time?"

"Yes, they have, and I think maybe you've known it, too."

I waited for more, but she was quiet.

"But isn't that really wrong? A scandal or a sin or something?"

"Well," Mother said, "you can look at it that way. Or you can see it as this town has chosen to see it. As one of Diane's gifts."

She offered me the cold cream. I sat on the bed for a while, then got up and hugged her goodnight. Her cheek was too greasy to kiss. "Yes," I said. "See you in the morning."

And that's just the way it was.

Five Rings

It wasn't turning out to be quite as glamorous as I'd imagined. Lady Capulet, a generous size 14 since her baby, had insisted we use a size 10 pattern for her costume. When we sewed up a rip in Mercutio's shirt, he snapped, "You've destroyed my character!" Five weeks into the summer, with *Romeo and Juliet* up and running and *Midsummer Night's Dream* in full rehearsal, I'd begun to understand that costumers—well, costume assistants, anyway—stood on the lower rung of the Asolo Theatre's ladder of prestige.

"Let's tell them to wash their own tights," Sylvia said, poking with her bare toes at the mass of sweaty hosiery the actors had left on the dressing room floor.

My new friend Sylvia was a city girl, by far my superior in sophistication and audacity. She'd seen her first play at age four, and, as a student at Chicago's Art Institute, had designed costumes for an impressive number of musicals and dramas. In the process, she had learned to regard actors as mobile mannequins, useful primarily if not exclusively for displaying the costumer's artistry.

I tried to copy Sylvia's worldly tone. "Well, we could leave the laundry to the lords and ladies, but then we'd be unemployed instead of downtrodden, and downtrodden at least gets us food and shelter." The very notion of Sylvia being downtrodden made me smile.

"Oh come on, Betty. It's summer in Sarasota. We can sit under an avocado tree and let the ripe fruit fall in our open hands."

"Can't do it," I said. "I lack your courage, your sense of adventure, and your trust fund. You will remember that in the fall, my fairy godmother turns me back into a mild-mannered, debt-ridden English scholar."

My personal history, which I kept mostly to myself, couldn't have been less like Sylvia's. I had grown up in Nowhere, North Carolina. I had read hungrily all my life because in my tiny town there was little else to do, and my knowledge of theatre came from the page, not the stage. My favorite English professor, hoping to broaden my limited horizons and knowing I made my own clothes, had urged me to apply for one of the Asolo's summer internships. Miraculously, I had been accepted, and I was hoarding every penny (I was pretty much paid in pennies) I earned.

Sylvia examined a false nail, which was coming loose. Then she kicked at the pile of tights and said, "We've got to do something to preserve our self-esteem. Let's take riding lessons."

From the moment we met, I'd been aware of the quick, hard current of Sylvia's personality. The first day on the job, she'd explained her life plan to the costume crew, which included the two of us and Jill, our dark-haired, deceptively languid boss. "Beginning this fall, I'm going to be the star student in some lucky and illustrious university graduate program, and very soon after that, you'll be reading about Sylvia Fielding, world famous costume designer."

Jill, who quietly harbored her own ambitions, had murmured, "That's very nice, Sylvia," and so a certain power struggle was born between them.

While the tights tumbled in the laundromat's heavy-duty dryer, we checked the ads section of the paper for a riding teacher. I thought Sylvia's antidote for diminished prestige was quirky, and, with my student loans, I really couldn't afford lessons of any kind, but I'd spent at least a third of my childhood reading Walter Farley's *Black Stallion* books and yearning for a pony, so I looked forward to sitting on a real live horse.

Later that morning, we learned that the director had approved Jill's sketches, and Sylvia and I spent an intense day pinning and basting the yards of rich fabric that would become costumes for the nobility in *Midsummer*. For me, there was magic in the process, and in the actors who transformed the plays from literature into life. During the rare lulls in the costume shop, I'd go up to the balcony to watch rehearsals. Each time Oberon said, "I know a bank where the wild thyme blows," he seemed truly more than mortal to me. When I tried to explain what I felt to Sylvia, she gave me a pitying look and warned me never to "gush" to the actors. "They'll think you fell off the turnip truck," she said.

Make that a tobacco truck and you'd not be far from wrong, I thought but didn't say.

That night after Jill released us, Sylvia scanned the newspaper ads, made some phone calls, and eventually wrote directions on a paper towel. The next morning before the Sarasota heat sat down hard, and long before late-rising Jill began work, we set out in Sylvia's car to locate our new riding teacher. Turning the car into a narrow, sandy driveway darkened by tall pines and palmettos, Sylvia said, "Well, he's cheap, and he sounded very old and very foreign on the phone, so he's probably one of those antique circus types that hang out around Ringling's winter quarters. We'll be his only students and he'll think we're gorgeous and extremely cool." She swerved to miss a Chihuahua in the middle of the drive barking till his eyes bulged dangerously. "Silly little thing," Sylvia said, "loud and conceited, like actors." She added, "Hope the horses are more impressive than the guard dog."

We parked in the fine blonde sand outside a weathered riding ring. More dark pines shaded half the ring and most of the yard in front of a long, low, green-roofed barn. At the corner of the first stall, a man rose slowly from a folding chair, pushing himself up on its aluminum arms. He wore jodhpurs, high brown riding boots, and a blue plaid Western shirt with pearl snaps. When we stood in front of him, he swept off his soft hat and held it at his waist. "Lay-dees," he said, "I am Captain Lawrence Meyer." I thought he looked like a character created by Jane Austen and Zane Gray.

Sylvia gave me a *so-what* look and held out her hand. A thin black man backed out of the second stall, carrying a shovel. "Bee," Captain Meyer said, "these are our new students, Miss Ferguson and Miss Fielding."

"Mornin'," Bee mumbled, looking as if he'd left out the "good" on purpose. To our teacher he said, "Lord God, Cap'n, it's hot already." He seemed unfazed by the fact that the Captain had given him no title and no last name. "Bee," said Captain Meyer, making the word puff out of his mouth, "don't let yourself be hot. Think of icebergs, think of snow drifts, and soon you will want a sweater."

"Yessir, Cap'n Meyer," said Bee, "I'm already shivering."

Sylvia widened her eyes at me and whispered, "Let's say we've got some serious laundry to do and split." But Bee was leading out two horses, saddled and ready to ride. And Captain Meyer was making us acquainted with them. They reminded me of the horses I had known and loved as a girl—Dan, the black Percheron, the ladies Margaret and Flash, and I was happy.

"This is Jer-ry," he announced, sweeping his arm toward a black and white paint with a long face. "Bet-ty, Jer-ry is your horse." He pronounced each syllable of each name. "And Syl-vi-a," he made the same courtly gesture toward a stocky chestnut, "you will ride Red."

Bee and Captain Meyer silently watched us mount, and Bee took us into the ring. Then he brought Captain Meyer's folding chair close to the railing. The Captain lowered himself into his seat, cleared has throat, and intoned, "Trrrot, Laydees, please ask your horses to trrrot," taking obvious pleasure in the roll of the word. The horses knew the command and took us round and round in a hard, unvarying gait. Bee shook his head and went back to his shovel. Captain Meyer, lulled by the regular hoof beats and the increasingly warm morning, soon dozed, waking at intervals to repeat his one-word instruction. When Sylvia and I had been thoroughly jarred and shaken, the Captain raised his hand and his voice and said, "Enough, Laydees. We don't want to tire the horses." And he called for Bee, who reappeared to take us back to the barn, where we dismounted to stand on trembling legs. Captain Meyer removed his hat, made a little bow, and said, "Good-bye, Laydees. I look forward to your return."

"Return, my Aunt Fanny," said Sylvia as she eased herself under the steering wheel. "That was no lesson, that was a torture session. And has he never heard of the Emancipation Proclamation? You'd think Bee was his slave."

"Well, he clearly does not see you and me as superior beings either. But I've got to go back. We've paid for six lessons, you know, and we have to see if he sleeps through every session." In fact, I'd had a fine time. Unlike Sylvia, who resisted all authority, I was comfortable in the familiar teacher/student hierarchy, and in spite of Jerry's jack-hammer trot, I'd liked being in a saddle, smelling horse sweat and warm pine needles instead of fabric sizing and laundry soap. Besides, I wanted to see the other horses that lived in Captain Meyer's infinitely long barn.

Sylvia recovered fast, and she'd taken a fancy to the somber Bee. "I'm going to make that man laugh," she vowed, as we parked in the alley behind the costume shop. That day, we started on the fairy costumes for *Midsummer*. Our fairies were the young sons of the theatre's patrons, and when they demanded to be called elves, we were obliged to oblige. After three long days of fitting wings and velvet tunics on small wriggling bodies, Sylvia and I were glad to drive through the bright morning sunlight and turn down the narrow drive again.

"Wait. Stop here," I said. "There's a horse loose. Let's get out. If we move slow, maybe we can drive him back to the barn."

"Whatever you say, Cowgirl," Sylvia said, and we moved apart, spread our arms wide and walked toward the tall sorrel clipping the stiff grass in the yard.

"Good morning, Laydees," called Captain Meyer from his folding chair. "Come and meet The Dutchman. But why are you walking strangely?" We dropped our arms and came forward to be formally introduced.

The Captain stood, spilling the Chihuahua from his lap. "Betty. And Sylvia. This is The Flying Dutchman. Perhaps you shouldn't stand too close." As if on cue, the horse laid back his ears and snaked his haughty head at Sylvia. "Shit," she said, ducking behind me. For an odd second, the power in our relationship shifted in my direction.

To me, Captain Meyer said, "Someday, Betty, when you learn to relax and keep your heels down, you will ride him."

I was honored and terrified. And I realized Captain Meyer had seen quite a lot between naps.

"Well, let me just say you're not putting me up on that high mean thing," Sylvia announced. "What keeps him from running away?"

"I do," said Captain Meyer, putting his hand on the red-brown back, almost the color of Romeo's costume. "My horses are at home here." He stood straighter and told us, "Sunrise is buried just under our feet."

Sylvia and I both stepped backward. "Sun who?" she asked.

"Come. Sit. We will ride soon." He gestured to a bench beside his chair. "I rode Sunrise in Ringling's center ring. He was a dressage horse, a dancing horse, all and completely golden. My wife, Natasha, is a dancer too. They danced side by side."

"Uh-huh," I heard Sylvia say under her breath, but I wanted more of this fabulous story, and pretended not to hear. The Captain continued, "I met her when I was training horses in Moscow." Bee appeared, nodded shortly to us, and brought out Red and Jerry.

As we rode into the ring, Captain Meyer gave the order to *Trot* with all the authority of Oberon making Puck promise to circle the earth in forty minutes. During our allotted half-hour, he gave us two pieces of instruction: "Sylvia, do not let your body flop" and "Betty, allow your horse to walk now and then." I would have been happy to let Jerry walk, but he wouldn't. Trot he'd been told to do, and trot he did. Sylvia, I felt sure, was trying hard not to flop.

"Come, come—enough for now," Captain Meyer announced as he opened the gate to the ring. "You may dismount and lead your horses to the barn."

A tanned woman had arrived during our lesson. She wore jodhpurs much like the Captain's except for the oval chamois inserts at the inseams, and a crisp white shirt with sleeves folded back twice on her forearms. It would have been a tough costume to make. Sylvia and I weren't introduced. Bee led out a horse from a distant stall—a horse of a different color and breed and bearing from Jerry and Red. She was gray with a light dapple and I knew from her far-set eyes and delicate ears that she was an Arabian, like the ones on the dust jackets of Walter Farley's books. She allowed Bee to put a bit in her proud mouth. Her regal bearing made The Dutchman, still cropping grass in the yard, look like a commoner.

"Cap'n Meyer's coaching them for the Olympics," Bee told us. Then I heard him mutter, "That old man taught God to ride."

"Well," said Sylvia, pushing a lock of her expensive haircut behind her ear so she could see to back the car, "I'm thinking two things. Our good Captain has delusions of past grandeur, and that snooty woman spends a bundle on clothes."

I decided not to "gush" about how dazzled I'd been by Captain Meyer's stories and by his striking student and her Arab mare. Glancing down at my own riding ensemble of jeans and cowboy boots, I said, "I guess I'm willing to be his charity case if I can find out what other horses he's got hidden in that long dark row of stalls."

"I have to find out how we're going to add gussets to Lady Capulet's red velvet gown without giving her a nervous breakdown," said Sylvia. "Us equestriennes are headed back to the sweat shop."

It wasn't really a sweat shop except when the moody air conditioner quit, as it did that very night. Jill, unfazed by the heat, was caught up in a creative frenzy. She twirled the end of her thick black braid, drew patterns, and, with what seemed to me wild abandon, sank her scissors into expensive velours and brocades. In this state, unlike her lesser assistants, she forgot about sleep. By 3 AM, I'd begun to be very afraid of the plunging needle in the industrial machine I was operating. As I fed it the cheap, heavy fabric for the costumes Bottom and the other low-lifes would wear, I imagined dark stitches running up my increasingly clumsy fingers. For Sylvia, being exhausted meant being crabby. In this state, like Mercutio, she would budge for no man's pleasure.

I could hear her in the cutting room badgering Jill again to pierce her ears.

"God, Jill, you wear those cheap Carmen clip-ons all the time. Why don't you cough up some of the big bucks you designers make, get your ears done, and buy some decent jewelry." I could imagine her touching her own 14 karat hoops. "That is, if you think you're woman enough to stand the pain."

Sylvia's sense of the appropriate, never strong, had completely expired. Wondering if Jill would retaliate, I stopped sewing to listen.

"Ummm," said Jill, zoned out on inspiration. "*Othello's* next. D'you think this color would make Desdemona look too pitiful?"

"You're scared and you'll never do it," Sylvia told our boss.

"Do what?"

"PIERCE YOUR EARS!" Sylvia shouted.

Jill came into the sewing room and unscrewed a needle from an idle machine. I followed her back to the full length mirror and watched her jab holes through both of her ear lobes. "Lend me your earrings, will you, Sylvia, till I can get some really good ones."

Wordless for once, Sylvia unfastened her gold hoops and handed them to Jill, who punched them in her bloody ears, wiped her fingers, and went back to the cutting table.

I wasn't sleepy anymore. When we quit, the sun was up.

By the time we got back to Captain Meyer's, Sylvia had recovered her brashness. "How old are you, anyway?" she asked our teacher, hands on her hips.

"Today, Sylvia, I am seventy-nine. When I feel not so well, I am eighty-four. Today is a young day." He was turning the pages of a heavy scrapbook, which he closed and held on his knees.

"And 'cause he feels young, he's gonna ride that hoss," muttered Bee. "That Dutchman. And I got to saddle that thing." He trudged off toward that duty.

"Sit, sit," said Captain Meyer, indicating a rough wooden bench. Then he handed the scrapbook to Sylvia. The clippings, brochures, and pictures proved that Captain Lawrence Meyer, former trainer of Moscow's famous Red Square horses, had performed in Ringling Bros. Barnum and Bailey's center ring on his peerless dancing stallion, Sunrise. In one picture, an erect and handsome Captain Meyer and his shimmering horse shared the spotlight with a ballerina in a classical costume and pose. "That's...? I asked.

"My wife, yes," and he told us the story of his friendship with Natasha's father, of the day in Moscow when his friend had begged the Captain to take his daughter, a young ballerina almost but not quite chosen by the Bolshoi, out of Russia. She was withering under the strict hierarchy of the Russian system.

"When I explained the difficulties, my friend said, 'Then marry her, only until she is free to dance.' She was eighteen and I was forty-one. We are married still."

On the last page of the scrapbook, a poster showed Captain Meyer, Sunrise, and Natasha taking a lavish bow in the center of the center ring. "In the circus," he told us, "the three of us were aristocracy."

We suddenly realized that, while the Captain finished his story, Bee had been holding the reins of a clearly restless Dutchman.

Soon, he was giving Captain Meyer a leg up on that hateful, beautiful horse. From the time they entered the ring, I didn't see the rider use a hand or a heel, but he made The Dutchman perform a controlled and elegant dance. I'd never seen dressage before. I could have watched all day.

"Enough," Captain Meyer announced. "He means well, but he is not Sunrise." Bee, half angry, half proud, held the horse steady as the Captain slowly swung his leg across the saddle and found the mounting block with his boot. This may have been one of his young days, but our teacher was clearly tired. "That was the lesson today," he told us. "Betty, do you understand how The Dutchman must be ridden? With firmness and certainty and kindness."

"I understand," I answered, and fervently hoped I did.

On the way back to town, Sylvia said, "Ok, it's a good sto-ry—good enough to make our lof-ty act-ors realize we exist." She separated the words in an imitation of Captain Meyer. "Poor babies. Make-believe's the only thing they understand." And that day, Mercutio, whose dangerous wit awed me onstage and off, sat on a stool in the sewing room and all but begged Sylvia to tell more about Captain Meyer and Sunrise.

Juliet seemed particularly interested in Sylvia's tale. Offstage, this woman, who called herself Linda Brittan, had no grace, no conversation, and no bosom. Sylvia pointed out that even when we sewed heavy padding in the bodice of her costume, the make-up people still had to paint on a cleavage. Onstage, however, her voice was rich caramel, her movements fluid. Each time she drank the Friar's potion in the Capulet's tomb, she became the epitome of bravery and faithfulness. When she asked, I was glad to give her Captain Meyer's phone number.

Wayne Manning, the tousled-haired company photographer, who, as far as I could tell never slept, also wanted to hear more about our discovery. He even talked vaguely about doing a photo story on Captain Meyer and Natasha. But Wayne's energies were too diffused to pursue that idea. He'd come by one night around 2 AM, red-eyed and wired, to tell us that he'd just slept with a woman whose mother had slept with Ernest Hemingway.

"Whatever we have to do for our fifteen minutes of fame," Sylvia told him.

When we arrived at Captain Meyer's for our next lesson, The Dutchman was doing a floating trot around the ring, and on his back was Linda Brittan.

"See," the Captain said, "your friend Juliet has come to ride. She is a natural, Laydees, so light, so straight."

All I could see was that Linda, at her first lesson, was riding The Dutchman, who was copper in the morning sun. I thought The Dutchman was a prize to be earned, that he would be my eventual reward for enduring Jerry's spine-slamming gait. Now it seemed that one star performer had recognized another and that Juliet had been promoted to the head of the class. Captain Meyer, registering my disappointment, said, "When you come again, Betty, The Dutchman will be your horse."

He remembered his promise. The next week, Sylvia took a picture of me as I sat on The Dutchman, looking tense and determined. But I had felt the sting of discrimination. I was sure that if I had been a leading lady instead of an assistant costumer, I would have been a natural too. For the first time, I wondered if

Sylvia was right about Captain Meyer. Maybe he was a proud old elitist who needed an audience to hear him brag about his past. The thought tumbled sharp and loose in my head.

Sylvia, too, was disgruntled by Captain Meyer's attention to Linda, but her real irritation came from another source. "I worked two whole days on that damn black and gold cape for Othello. You remember, I cut the pattern, found that luscious lining. And did Jill, the goddess of design, give me one breath of credit? When that new director said it was perfect, she smiled her very sweet and sexy smile and said, 'We aim to please.' There's no *we* in that cape. It's mine. Not that anyone will ever know."

I muttered commiseration. Sylvia stewed some more. Then she said, "To hell with costuming. I'm going to join the circus. I found this guy who used to be a clown and he's going to give us trapeze lessons. I'm paying if you'll stand under me when I fall." I thought of saying *No*, but I couldn't make the sound, so I nodded and hung on for the ride, flotsam on the tide of my friend's shifting ambitions.

And so, Thursday on our lunch break, during the hottest, most humid part of the day, Sylvia and I began to learn the still trapeze.

Another ad in the paper had led my dauntless friend to arrange lessons for two with Bill (I never learned his last name; he wouldn't take checks, just cash), who'd been a Ringling clown for fifteen years. When I asked her what a clown knew about teaching trapeze, Sylvia explained that Bill had married a featured trapeze artist ("I married up," he told us later, grinning) and he acted as her trainer. We met her twice, a small, long-muscled woman who honored us with a cool smile. Bill, whose flexible face must have been a good palette for clown make-up, was a much more active teacher than Captain Meyer. That first day, he had us climb slats nailed into a live oak tree, to a bar suspended by thick ropes from a perfectly horizontal limb, and hang by our knees for a slow count of thirty. My head felt like a thick pot which had collected all the blood in my body. Then we climbed down the tree—and directly back up again to repeat the procedure. Four times. At the end of our lesson, we sat on a rough board bench, much like the one at Captain Meyer's, our legs as palsied from our efforts as they had been the first day we'd ridden Red and Jerry, and heard Bill's evaluation: "You're stronger, Betty (I tried not to look proud) but Sylvia's more determined."

"Damn right," said Sylvia. "Soon you'll be reading about Sylvia Fielding, world famous trapeze artist."

In the next few weeks, we opened a lavish version of *Midsummer* which emphasized the tension between the noble lords and ladies and the hard-handed laborers, and turned our efforts to *Othello*. When we weren't sewing new costumes or washing old ones, we were either riding a horse or hanging from a trapeze. Bill soon had us doing forms on the bar in the tree—holding on by ankles and hands and bending ourselves into a lopsided "O," stomach side out, or suspending ourselves by one ankle and the opposing hand while the free hand arced out in a circus "ta-da."

I held my own until the lesson when we hung by our heads from a heavy loop that passed over our ears and around the back of our neck. That exercise made me drunk and blind. Sylvia got as far as trying, unsuccessfully, to dangle from a short, soft bar which she held in her teeth. "Don't worry," Bill said, "you'll get the hang of it," and waited for us to laugh.

Then, as further comfort, he explained to Sylvia that she'd be one among many still trapeze performers and that even in a spangled leotard, almost no one would be looking at her. Only the big stars, like his wife, got the crowd's attention. He admitted that the same was true of clowns. "We're mostly filler," he said, "just noise and color to occupy the gaps between the main acts. If the tigers ate a few of us, nobody would care."

There was no bitterness in Bill, though, and when we asked him if he knew Captain Meyer, he said, "Know of, sure. Old hands still talk about him and that golden horse. But we don't exactly travel in the same circles."

"Well, that's dumb," Sylvia announced. "You're both circus guys, you're both teachers. We'll just get you together."

"Yeah," said Bill, making an odd smile. "Now let me see one more double ankle drop from each of you, and make it proud and flashy."

The night *Othello* opened, Sylvia and I arrived at the theatre two hours before curtain, anticipating the chaos of clothing as jittery actors struggled into their doublets and hose. High-born Juliet, transformed now into the servant Emelia, rose in my estimation by thanking us for her costume. Othello, an imposing actor with high-gloss black skin and a bass drum voice, wore Sylvia's robe as if gold brocade was his everyday attire—and left it, at the end of the play, flung over his dressing room chair. Feeling Sylvia's influence, I thought of the distance between this arrogant, accomplished man and Bee, the other black person I knew that summer. I wondered if they'd like to have dinner together.

At the end of our next riding lesson—no Juliet, no Olympic hopeful; just us Lay-dees—Sylvia informed Captain Meyer that we were learning the trapeze. His response was to make his eyes big and his mouth small. "The still trapeze, of course," Sylvia continued. "A really neat man is teaching us. He's a clown with Ringling, and you'd like him. Maybe we can bring him out...."

"No, Sylvia," said Captain Meyer. "You know very little about the circus. There are levels of people. Clowns are at the bottom. Clowns and center ring performers do not meet."

He couldn't have been more direct or less angry, and the subject couldn't have been more closed. He motioned to Bee to take Red and Jerry back to their stalls, made us a little bow, and said, "Until our next lesson."

Sylvia's Volvo swerved down the dirt drive. "That old bigot," she yelled, stomping on the gas for emphasis. She was mad, I thought, partly because of Captain Meyer's reaction and partly because he'd dismissed us before she could think of a comeback. "'Levels of people,'" she stormed. "Let them just try to put me on a level. I'll tear that big top down." All the way to the costume shop, Sylvia railed against the Captain. "He used to be in the circus, he used to be a star. Now he sits in a plastic chair and watches women bounce around that everlasting ring. And that makes him high lord god superior?!?"

And then I made a discovery. I didn't want Sylvia's attitude, ambition, or anger. I'd gladly accept the actors' foibles in exchange for the magic they made on stage; that they were mortals and, sometimes, fools did not diminish that magic. And Captain Lawrence Meyer, with his horses and stories of horses, had made me see the center ring of the Greatest Show On Earth. In return, I freely granted him his pride and prejudice. I was no turnip: I knew that William Faulkner was a world-class binge drinker, and William Shakespeare had abandoned his wife in Nowhere on Avon for the London stage, and they both had written words that rang around the world. I could tell the dancer from the dance.

Bill listened, the next morning, with a half-smile as Sylvia, hands on hips, sputtered about Captain Meyer's rudeness. "I could have saved you the trouble," he told her, "but it was sweet of you to try." Then he handed her a thick white envelope, "Here's your contract, girl. You're going to have a bird's eye view of how the circus works."

The next couple of weeks were frantic. The full repertoire was up and running, and on Wednesdays and Saturdays, matinee days, Jill helped Sylvia and me with the great bags of laundry and the constant repairs to snaps and braid and plumes. As Sylvia and Jill laughed at the amount of aromatic sweat produced by the "thes-bi-ans," Sylvia's new term for the actors, the tension in the costume shop lessened, and Jill asked concerned questions about Sylvia's plan to join the circus. I wondered if she liked Sylvia better because they were no longer competitors.

When we finally got back to the now-familiar riding ring, Captain Meyer greeted us effusively—"A pleasure, Laydees." Sylvia merely grunted. Bee returned the grunt as he brought out Red and Jerry. Apparently, The Dutchman had been a one-time thing. I didn't mind; I was far less tense on a plebian mount. As we drove away from the stable after an hour of trotting, Sylvia said, "I'm not going back. I've learned precious little, except that Red and Captain Meyer are both pains in the butt. I do hate that I never made Bee laugh, though."

There followed a period of frenzy, full of the glory and tedium of running three of Shakespeare's plays in repertory. Audiences rose in standing ovations, costumes ripped and were repaired. Wayne Mooring and Linda Brittan, the photographer and Juliet, got married one weekend, and there was general disagreement about which of them had lost prestige in the union. Sylvia got a plum of a teaching assistantship at Cooper Union and tore up her circus contract. "One of my very dumbest ideas," she told Jill and me as she pointedly admired Othello's cape.

Then the summer was gone—sets struck, costumes stored, goodbyes said. Sylvia phoned Bill to explain her new plan, and she told us what he said: "Probably best. You've got better things to do with your life than hang around the circus." I didn't say goodbye to Captain Meyer. I told myself that I had no time and no way to get back to the stables. I thought of calling, but there was either too much or not enough to say. So my last act in Sarasota was to walk downtown to the stationery store and, in Sylvia's honor, buy the most expensive card I could find. On it I wrote, "I am so grateful to you, Captain Meyer, for all I learned this summer." I was glad that it was true.

Lessons

It was 2:45 PM on a Monday, fifteen minutes before the last bell. I stood in front of the classroom, cradling the heavy anthology in my crossed arms, taking inventory of my students' faces—those I could see. The heads of those who'd worked, or partied, late the night before were sinking toward their desks. Some faces were in profile, alert to the significant rustles and whispers in the room. On others, furtive smiles came and went, suggesting a remembered joke, an anticipated date. No one, I knew beyond doubt, was paying attention to Tennyson. Except, of course, for Tom.

These were not bad kids. A consolidation of small rural high schools had brought them together in the unimaginatively named Western High School for what would be, for many, their last year of formal education. They had been as kind to me as their interests allowed. The girls asked me where I got my hair cut—possibly so they could avoid the establishment; the boys wanted to know what gas mileage I got in my old silver Volvo. I was afraid they pitied me because I was married and therefore had no real future and because I loved, and wanted them to love words that people had written so long ago.

The commencement speaker at my college graduation the year before had urged my class to "Go and burn with a hard, gem-like flame." And I had tried, was trying. I still believed I could ignite, inspire the sloppy, sleepy seniors in my classroom, could make them understand that literature was pertinent—no, crucial—to their lives. But they looked on this great gift I was offering as an abacus, a quill pen, cod liver oil—strange, outdated, and useless. "Send my roots rain," I had muttered as the class began.

I had hoped that Tennyson's "Charge of the Light Brigade," whose soldiers had died because "Someone had blundered," would seem current to them, as it did to me, that they would hear the screams and smell the gunpowder, protest the terrible waste; instead, they rolled their eyes and groaned. "You got to know, Ms. Moffett," said Emily of the sky-blue contacts, "that old stuff's got nothing to do with us." Earl, less of a diplomat, had said simply, "A bunch of this poetry is about nature. I hate nature." They *had* responded to one line from "Flower in a Crannied Wall." "Hey Debbie," Gene had shouted, "Let me pluck you out of the crannies!" making "pluck" sound like a familiar four-letter word.

At the beginning of the semester, for a brief, heady time, they'd seemed to like *Beowulf.* True, with the exception of Tom, they ignored the themes of loyalty and honor. The boys, especially, treated the Anglo-Saxon chronicle like a particularly violent comic book. Cody had stopped me in the hall to say, "Hey, Ms. Moffett, didn't you think it was cool when old Grendel ate those guys while they were sleeping, their hands and feet and everything, and then old Bear Wolf tore his arm off?!"

Never mind. Close enough. I rejoiced that they'd absorbed the story and translated it into their own experience. And I celebrated the connection, though partial and temporary, between their world and mine.

Chaucer, however, had been a disaster. I'd pushed the Wife of Bath's bawdiness as much as I dared, the ardent church-goers, who made up most of the community, being always on red alert. I'd explained that the Wife had been married five times, and was looking forward to her sixth husband, who she hoped would be meek and lusty. "Can't you just see her, hear that brassy laugh?" I'd asked. "No," Debbie said, and added, "Sorry." And Earl had summed up the class opinion: "Why couldn't that Chaucer just speak English?"

But today, Monday, began a new week, and today was Keats, and there, as always, every day, was Tom. He sat in the second seat of the second row, and he got it—all of it. I tried not to look at this slender boy too often because I didn't want to blow his cover, to make him guilty among his peers of understand-ing—and liking—this literature stuff. When I allowed myself to look his way, I found, among the drooping, doodling students, a face alive and aware. I didn't mind that he seldom spoke. He let me know by small nods and smiles that he felt the words as I did. And occasionally, for my sake, he risked detection. He'd managed to amuse his classmates and his teacher by venturing that Hamlet wouldn't make much of an action figure. And, more recently, when the others had declared themselves terminally bored by Wordsworth's golden daffodils, Tom had said quietly, "I've been there."

For weeks, I'd comforted myself by imagining how Tom would love Keats. I'd even allowed myself to hope that the other students would respond to the sumptuous love story in "The Eve

106

of St. Agnes," my own favorite. How could they not? The story was made for them, out of their own daydreams: Boy meets girl; girl's family hates boy; boy and girl elope. At least, everyone would recognize the plot. And Tom would appreciate the language, the images, the soul of the poem. It was a gift I could give him, a gift he would accept and remember with gratitude.

I could tell right away that the weekend had made unusual demands on my seniors. They seemed to try at first, to respond in some way to my almost desperate enthusiasm. But heads slipped off the props of hands, eyes fluttered, snapped open—closed.

"Look," I begged (I knew I was begging), "Madeline, this beautiful young girl, has just left a huge party, and she's standing in her bedroom. Her dress has so many jewels on it that it stands up by itself when she takes it off."

"God," I heard Ellen whisper to Frankie. "Poor Madeline. How'd she dance?" At least she was listening.

"And remember," I pushed on, "The boy who loves her is in the closet watching all this." I was in dangerous territory again, but I didn't care. "And Keats wants us to feel and smell and taste as well as look. He says, 'She unclasps her warmed jewels one by one.' See, her necklace has been lying against her throat, her... chest." I wished I could say "bosom" or "breast." That would open their eyes.

But I got nothing. Except for one snicker and the soft burr of Carl's snore. Well, I turned to Tom.

Tom had hidden most of his face with his hand. Head, shoulders, his knees under the desk, were all turned away from me. He was more absent than if he had not come to class. I felt a terrible tiredness. I shut the book softly and sat down at my desk.

The weight of my disappointment kept me silent for the last few minutes of the class. When Debbie asked, "You ok, Ms. Moffett?" I nodded but didn't speak. The bell rang and students shuffled sleepily into the hall. Tom, who still hadn't looked at me, was the last to go. I said his name and he turned slowly around.

"Didn't you like it at all?" I asked. "Didn't it...."

He answered with his eyes down. "Ms. Moffett, I'm seventeen years old. That stuff in the poem—it's all I ever think about. I just can't use any more of it." He raised his eyes and his hand, and walked quietly out the door.

I opened the book and brought it close to my face, too close to read. I thought I could smell candles, incense, hear the rustle of a brocade gown. I knew that Tom had heard it, too.

Believers

Manteo, in the mid 1960s, was a small, practical island you had to pass over on the way to Nags Head, its rowdier, more glamorous neighbor. Houses on Manteo were built short and flat to duck the hurricanes that whipped the North Carolina shore. The island's residents worked hard at logical jobs—fishing, crabbing, shrimping—and the smell of bait, shells, and fish innards was strong and permanent.

The atmosphere of eastern North Carolina seemed to breed ghosts and legends. Carrie and I knew the stories from our mothers, who had been reared a few miles inland, on the flat, rich coastal soil. We knew about Chat and Thomas, slave and master, who a hundred years before, had fought until both men died a bloody death, and who now appeared on stormy nights as fireballs crashing into each other in the sky. And the spirit of the pirate Blackbeard, his beard adorned with lit candles, we knew stalked the sandy island in search of treasure he had buried there long ago. And lest we forget, the mystery of the vanished group of English settlers who disappeared from Manteo 300 years in the past, Paul Green's outdoor drama, *The Lost Colony*, had been playing nightly every summer for twenty-five years—since its opening in 1937. It was exciting stuff. Sir Walter Raleigh and Queen Elizabeth made appearances, Indians shot fire arrows, and Virginia Dare discreetly and tastefully became the first English baby born in the New World.

Actors and technicians came from all over North Carolina to be in the drama. Theatre majors from the state's colleges and universities typically got the substantial roles of Sir Walter and Her Majesty as well as the other speaking parts. This particular summer, Randy McPherson, a halfback on the UNC football team and a member of the Carolina Playmakers, was playing the role of Wanchese, fierce chief of the Roanoke Native American tribe. Every night, he got to threaten Sir Walter Raleigh: "When moon come big, white man be gone." Music and dance departments provided performers in those areas, locals filled in as extra Indians and colonists, and one night each summer, the newest baby in Manteo, regardless of gender, played Virginia Dare.

In this setting of real and make-believe, a group of us from "the drama," (as the islanders called it) gathered after a performance at Drinkwater's Folly, the oldest house on the island. Built a hundred years before by a Captain Drinkwater, it had a half-hearted elegance—two stories, porches on three sides, and high ceilings. Hal and Cynthia Eilert, hardworking university professors in the winter, beachcombing members of the *Lost Colony* choir in the summer months, were living in the house. Their three young daughters were asleep upstairs.

"Now we all know that absolutely nothing may happen here tonight." John Clarke spoke in his deep, reasonable voice. "I look on this as a kind of experiment. I'm just curious to see what we as a group, in this place so steeped in history and mystery, might—sorry—conjure up."

Carrie, sitting beside me in the circle, leaned over and whispered, "That smart-talking man can call this whatever he wants to. I know what we're doing. We're having a séance. And I'm going to be possessed."

It was exactly midnight. We were sitting on the living room floor. A single lit candle burned in the dead center of our circle. John Clarke had convened the meeting. Scholar, actor, and amateur hypnotist, he had been cast for the summer as the garrulous Governor John White. Before going on with his introduction, he glanced at Carrie, and I wondered if he'd heard her comment. My cousin was, as always, unfazed.

John continued. "My old friends Cynthia and Hal have generously allowed us to use this house, which—did you know?—was a makeshift Confederate hospital just about a century ago. In another act of generosity, Cynthia, who delivered all three of her girls under hypnosis and is extremely sensitive to hypnotic suggestion, has agreed to test the atmosphere for us."

I looked around the circle. On my right, Sandy, my sane, steady husband of one year, and the current stage manager for *The Lost Colony*, looked skeptical. I regarded him as buffer and shield for whatever the spirit world might bring forth. With the exception of John, Hal, and Cynthia, everyone else looked more or less wild-eyed, including—no, especially—Carrie, who was visiting for the weekend. She was seated on my left. My cousin was a believer, a conduit, and I knew that anything dramatic or dangerous would come straight through her. Other candle-lit faces included those of my fellow choir members, a dozen or so colonists, and four or five Indian dancers, still wearing traces of terra cotta make-up from the evening's performance. I noticed that cast members from the island were not represented, though John had made the invitation general. Was it because the natives didn't believe in this hocus-pocus, or because they did?

"All right," said John, "Let's just join hands and sit quietly. No, wait. Sorry. Please be sure you're not sitting beside anyone you know well."

Reluctantly, I stood up and looked around the circle. Carrie had already found a position between two receptive-looking actors. I took a seat between the prop master and a thin, dark-haired dancer named Allen, who whispered, "This is a bunch of crap, but nobody'd come drinking."

"Now," said John, "I'll turn out the overhead light. Let's join hands again and shut our eyes. Quiet, please, and try to be open to anything."

A jolt went through the circle when the front door banged and Paul made his entrance. I wondered if he'd been waiting on the porch. Paul Marshall was Carrie's current boyfriend, a hard-drinking, land-owning frat boy from a small eastern North Carolina town that bore his family's name. He had a practical business major and a penchant for practical jokes—just the type to be attracted to my daring cousin. In fact, every type was attracted to Carrie, and she treated each romance as a new adventure. Paul, I figured, was one in the series. His Oxford cloth shirt and Weejun loafers made an odd contrast to the prevalent garb of leotards and dashikis, but for Paul, "out of place" was something that happened to other people. He grinned and gestured, two people made room between them, and he became part of the circle. John repeated his instructions, and we sat in silence for what seemed like a very long time.

"Open your eyes, please." I had peeked once, and found Sandy watching me, Carrie concentrating intently, and Paul seeming to nod. The circle was quiet, and John prompted, "Did anyone experience anything at all?"

A minute more of silence, and Becky, a young colonist, said, "Well, it probably wasn't anything, but just for a second, I thought I felt something cold right behind me."

Two others murmured, "So did I."

John waited for other responses and then asked, "Can you say if what you felt was friendly or angry?"

"Not friendly," said Becky, and no one else spoke.

"Cynthia," said John, "Are you willing…."

"Yes," she replied.

This mother of three, this no-nonsense, thirty-something teacher of music theory, was way at the top of the maturity scale in our gathering. We would believe what she said.

John spoke a few calm words to her, and her posture changed. Back straight, hands soft in her lap, she said clearly, "There is a strong and harmful presence in this room tonight. It does not want us here."

I heard the shush of in-drawn breath and one whisper. John spoke more soft words to Cynthia, and then addressed us all.

"We have to decide together," he said. "Should we continue or stop? We may be getting into something…."

"Go on, go on," said several voices. One of them was Carrie's. Two people got up and quietly left. Hal went upstairs to the girls' bedroom.

"That's good," John said. "No one should stay who feels uncomfortable or afraid. And please, now is the time for anyone who doesn't believe in this process to leave. The presence of a skeptic will keep whatever's here from coming closer—or make it angrier still."

I looked at Alan, the doubting dancer. He'd lost some of his sneer. I looked at Paul. During the brief time I'd known him, he had made several points clear: He scorned non-drinkers, non-hunters, and non-Democrats. He particularly scorned the airy-fairy world of The Theatre. And he enjoyed making his views known to any kind of audience. His presence made me tense. I looked at Sandy, who raised an eyebrow. I knew he was a first-class non-believer. I also knew he was curious—and a drama major and budding playwright—and that he was leaving the decision to me. Then Alan shrugged and offered his hand. I took it and the "experiment" resumed.

This time John put out both the light and the candle, and gradually, in the darkness and silence, which had thickened somehow, I heard Alan's breathing change. "Asleep," I thought, and waited for his hand to relax. Instead it tightened on mine and began to twist and pull. I considered letting go. It would have been easy; both our hands were slick with sweat. *But if I'm holding this hand*, I figured, *at least I know where it is.* Then, Alan began to whisper and to make a sound between a purr and a groan.

When John lit the candle, Alan was staring straight ahead. He turned his rounded eyes to me and said softly, "Listen, my father? He's been dead three years. He was here. Here. And he told me, 'Leave, boy, if you know what's good for you.' You can stay

114

if you want to, but you're crazy if you do." And in one efficient movement, he was up and out the door.

I took advantage of the general disruption to reposition myself beside Sandy. I had just finished my BA at Chapel Hill, where I'd given up superstition. But my mother still read palms, and claimed kin with Blackbeard. If there were unfriendly presences abroad, I did not want to become their intimate, but I didn't want to miss them either. Across the room, I saw Paul beckon to Carrie, who shook her head and stayed put. Caution had been left out of Carrie's make-up, and she was ready to play hostess to any spirit, whatever its intent.

Lighting the candle again, John reminded us, "We can stop at any point, you know. If any one feels threatened, just speak up." But the brew of excitement, dread, and anticipation had become potent enough to make protest unlikely, if not impossible. We joined hands and were silent again. Some small groans and gasps began to issue from the circle. Someone said a breathy "Nooo," and someone else sighed, "Please."

A scream made the whole circle go rigid. Except on the stage, I had never heard a man scream before, and my heart paused and then bumped like a drum. The man began to speak.

"Don't do it. Don't. It hurts too bad."

Whose voice? Not one I recognized. Or did I? Sandy squeezed my hand to let me know it wasn't him.

The voice became louder, and piteous. "Stop them. Don't let them do it."

Someone shouted, "Turn on the lights," and several voices answered, "NO."

Then the man's voice, hysterical now. "Not my leg. Don't let them take my leg."

And Carrie said, "Paul?"

John turned on the lights, and Paul was writhing on the floor, holding his right thigh with both hands. Carrie knelt beside him, touching his face. "It's all right, Baby," she said, over and over.

Paul opened his eyes, sat up, and looked around the broken circle. He seemed to be searching for something familiar. The rest of us stared at him and then looked away. What had we witnessed? Were we guilty of something?

Then John spoke from across the room, his voice deep and calm. "Paul, you're safe now. Can you tell us what happened?"

"I...." Paul started, cleared his throat, began again. "I was a soldier, a rebel soldier, and I'd been shot. Four or five guys were holding me down, and somebody who looked like a doctor had a saw in his hand." He stopped.

"Don't make him tell it," Carrie said.

"No, I can," said Paul. "All I know is that they were going to take off my leg." He stretched out his right leg, making sure of its wholeness.

"Thank you for telling us," John said. Then to the rest of us: "We've done enough for tonight. We should all go home now."

Gradually, people got to their feet. Few spoke. Someone thanked Cynthia, as if we'd been having a dinner party. Someone else pushed open the door, hesitated, and went out.

Sandy, Carrie, and I walked Paul to his car. He was limping a little when he got in.

Carrie, in a rush of concern and curiosity, said, "Paul, what was it like? Did it hurt bad? Do you remember?"

Paul rested his forehead on the steering wheel. His shoulders began to shake.

"Oh Paul, I'm so sorry," Carrie said, and knelt beside him. "I never wanted…."

Sandy took a step toward the car to offer comfort. And then Paul raised his head. He was grinning.

"Paul," Carrie said, standing up. "Did you…. Paul Marshall, were you pretending?"

"Not pretending, Shug," Paul said. "Acting. Somebody had to show these high-toned thes-bi-ans how to act."

Coming Clean

My earliest memory of Granny's house has to do with reaching for a piece of Aunt Rosser's coconut cake. I must have been four, and my action was automatic, like breathing or blinking. The cake was deep yellow with heavy white frosting; the coconut was moist, sweet, and perfect for falling on the floor. In a movement every bit as reflexive as mine, Cousin Russ, twice my age, produced a sheet of newspaper from the neat stack in the pantry, folded it twice, and held it under my hands to catch the crumbs of cake and coconut that threatened the spotless kitchen linoleum. Like all the Fergusons, Russ hated a mess.

I had been born into a family that did cry over spilt milk. A broken dish was a calamity, spilled sugar a character flaw. Maybe it came from our Scotch heritage, or generations of trying to plow straight rows in North Carolina's red clay soil. Whatever the reason, a mess depressed and disgusted every Ferguson I ever knew. They liked things neat, orderly, familiar, predictable, and clean. Evidence of these traits was everywhere in Granny's kitchen. When the family gathered on weekends, brown paper bags were taped underneath and behind the electric skillet to catch the pops of grease from the chicken Aunt Hayes always fried. The rinse water for the dishes was hot enough to cook shrimp.

This careful care extended far beyond the house. In the yard, the grass had to be mowed in a pattern Uncle Charles had established years ago. Every fence post was straight and sturdy, every strand of barb wire taut. Once, when Cousin Ed failed to fasten the gate exactly right, the cows got out and knocked over Granny's scuppernong grapevines. Daddy and Uncle Charles didn't speak to Ed for two years.

Growing up among these people was frightening—and wonderful. Their eccentricities produced grand dramatic stories, which they told over and over, never quite the same way. Most of them had to do with someone—never a Ferguson—creating a mess, and someone else—a Ferguson every time—tidying up. Daddy said that all the way back to Great Grandpa Joe McDonald, the family had been "quare" about order and cleanliness. They agreed that anyone who didn't hold the same notion was morally inferior.

After Granny died, the family continued to gather at the farm. In my teens, I spent hours walking through its woods and rolling pastures. I knew that the man I would someday marry would have to love this place. It wouldn't be hard—the land was beautiful. But he'd also have to love the Fergusons. That would be harder. The real challenge, of course, would be finding a man my family would love—or at least accept.

I found him, I fervently hoped, in a drama class at the university. The Fergusons did not like the university; they regarded it as a convening place for people with messily liberal views. I had risked their disapproval to go there. Now I wanted them to meet and be kind to a man who embraced those views, whose family they did not know, and whose major course of study was—Theatre. On the way to Granny's, I jittered with nerves:

"You'll remember to wipe your feet, won't you, Sandy, and not let flies in the screen door?"

"I sure will—I mean, won't," he replied, smiling.

Sandy wasn't really opposed to cleanliness, but sometimes he failed to take it seriously.

Only Aunt Hayes and Mama were in the house when we arrived. Mama was easy, but she wasn't really a Ferguson. She loved everybody who didn't bite or spit on the floor, and my handsome, gentle Sandy didn't do either. Aunt Hayes was tougher, but she nodded slightly when Sandy scraped his shoes on the doormat before coming up on the porch. We chatted and drank iced tea for a few minutes. Then Sandy did what a man was supposed to do. "Miss Hayes," he said, "would you mind if I get my gun and walk down in those woods behind the house? I've got a feeling I might find some quail using in there."

"That's all right," she said, "but you'll get those city shoes filthy."

"Thank you, Ma'am, I've got boots in the car." He shut the screen door quietly and firmly, just as I'd coached him.

Mama smiled and squeezed my hand. Aunt Hayes said, "He seems decent. Where'd you say he was from?"

Pride wrestled with caution and won. I wanted to brag about Sandy, and I thought his missionary parents would impress her. "Well, he was born in China, Aunt Hayes," I said.

Her mouth turned down. "Huh," she snorted, "I knew there was something funny about his eyes."

I hoped Sandy would remember to change his boots when he got back. I hoped he'd wash his hands before dinner and help clear the table afterwards. I hoped being really, really clean would make up for the peculiarity of starting his life outside of North Carolina.

During our courtship and the early years of our marriage, Sandy made progress with my family. From that first day, he loved the farm. Hunting its woods and fishing its ponds taught him more about the land than I would ever know. And somewhere, maybe backstage in the theatre, he'd learned to use tools and tinker with motors. He, Daddy, Uncle Charles, and the cousins spent chunks of the weekends observing and critiquing the carpenters down the hill who were building a tiny, perfect vacation house for Aunt Nina and Uncle Tinky. My men were happier still with their hands deep in the entrails of the newish Farmall or the 1948 Farmall Cub. This particular tractor needed frequent and special care; its radiator had to be flushed out every month or so. "Quare," Daddy said, "just like the rest of us." All the men wore dark green coveralls to keep the grease and gas off their clothes. When the machinery was running again, they shucked their outer garments like dirty skins and hung them on hooks in the pump house. I couldn't tell Sandy's coverall from the others'—a good sign, I reckoned.

A relief, too, because in ways even stranger than his foreign birth, Sandy was different from the Fergusons. He had traveled far outside the Old North State. He had been in the army (good), where he had studied Russian (Oh, Lord!). And then there was his job—he taught acting and directing in a nearby college. My family approved of education, but putting on plays? Wasn't acting just a jumble of pretending? Was it even moral? And so, Sandy's profession was rarely mentioned, as if it were a chronic sickness, or a misdemeanor.

But even harder for the Fergusons to deal with was Sandy's attitude toward a mess.

One unusual weekend when all the motors worked and no fences were down, Uncle Charles and Daddy decided to fix what might someday be a hole in the roof. *A stitch in time*, they said, and *Never put off till tomorrow*. My uncle, who feared nothing else, hated heights, and Daddy knew exactly how to hold a ladder steady, so Sandy was elected to do the actual patching. A bucket of nails on one arm, shingles tucked under the other, a hammer in the loop of his coveralls, he began his ascent. Daddy was already coaching: "Now the problem's right at the edge there," when the sixth rung of the ladder snapped. Nails, shingles, and Sandy went everywhere. The older men were genuinely worried that Sandy might be hurt. He wasn't, much. Then they took in the disarray—the broken ladder, the refuse strewn around the yard—and the gloom began to gather. Like a Greek chorus, Daddy and Uncle Charles chanted, "Those old nails will wreck the mower." "Every one of the shingles broke." "Watch now, it'll rain for sure."

Shaking his head, Daddy turned back to Sandy. "Say, your coverall's torn. I'll bet you're hurt somewhere. That would just about cap the whole thing...." He stopped. Sandy was laughing.

"Wow, what an event. We should have had a bigger audience," he said, testing an ankle and rubbing a hip—and laughing.

I'd been down the hill to check the progress on Aunt Nina's nearly completed Little House, and when I walked up on this scene, I was pretty sure my uncle and father were about to kill my husband. Sandy quickly realized his mistake, and in absolute silence, the three of them began to pick up nails. Finally, Uncle Charles made a sound between a snort and a laugh and said, "I hope you know, Boy, you broke my best ladder." I knew the worst danger had passed. The story of Sandy messing up the roof project would pass into Ferguson folklore.

Such lapses kept Sandy on probation. It was well and properly noted that he didn't mind driving a dirty car and that he once brought a live possum, nastiest of animals, into Granny's yard. But he enjoyed a friendly game of poker, often bought Daddy's favorite brand of bourbon, knew about hunting and guns, and was consistently good to me. These things won favor from my family. And when our son Ruben came along, Sandy was good to him as well. Daddy found Ruben fascinating: "Look at him reach for that chicken leg," he'd say at the dinner table. "See how those little hands work." Then he'd use his clean napkin to wipe every speck of grease off those little hands. Since the aunts and cousins liked the newest family member, and Mama and Ruben were very best friends, I figured we'd been woven into the Ferguson fabric.

Proof of this acceptance came one weekend when everybody had gathered at Granny's. Chicken was frying, cakes and pies were baking, tractors were humming, and space was scarce. Daddy took me aside and put his hand on my shoulder. "Betty, he said, "Nina and Tinky are going home tonight. They said you could stay in the Little House."

"All three of us?" I wanted to be sure.

123

"Yes, you'll have to be mighty careful. You know how Nina is."

I thought, *That's the pot speaking of the kettle*, but I understood. Aunt Nina had the full dose of Ferguson finicky-ness, plus lots of taste and a little money. She and Uncle Tinky had furnished their tiny house with pottery, oil lamps, and old prints—all handsome, all carefully chosen, all fragile. I was touched by their offer, and scared to death. What if we broke something? I knew Daddy was thinking the same thing.

That evening, we eased Ruben's folding crib through the front door, being careful not to nick the Williamsburg Blue door frame. We noted the dustless walnut table, the matched seams of the wallpaper, the pristine counter tops. We did not feel at home.

But later that night when Ruben was sweetly asleep, Sandy and I made a fire (we'd sweep up the ashes later) and poured two glasses of wine (we'd wash the glasses in scalding water). We put our feet up on the antique trunk, and quickly took them down. Finally, we relaxed. It was a beautiful Little House.

The next morning, we got up early, drank coffee and washed the cups, fed Ruben and vacuumed the floor. We stripped the bed and folded the sheets. Pretty soon, we figured, someone—Daddy, Uncle Charles, one of the cousins—would be down to say "Good morning," and to inspect the house.

I opened the bedroom closet to make sure we hadn't left a dirty sock and was surprised to see a rifle propped in the corner. "Sandy," I said, "why in the world is this here?"

"Don't know. Tinky doesn't hunt. I expect he keeps it here to warn off stray possums."

"Or stray people," I said. "There're some pretty valuable pieces in this place. That thing's not loaded, is it?"

"I'm sure not." Sandy, lover of all guns, lifted this one carefully out of the closet. "It shouldn't be," he said, picking up the gun and swinging it away from us. "I'll just check."

Somehow—reflex? fate?—his finger touched the trigger and a sharp, crisp blast filled the house. I didn't scream. Ruben didn't cry. We all were still until the noise was completely gone. Then it was hard to think of what to say.

"What did it hit?" I asked.

"The wall," Sandy answered.

I expected to see a huge and jagged gap, but we had to look hard to find the hole, all but invisible in the pattern of the wallpaper. Then we were still again, waiting to see if water or sparks would spray out of the hole.

I began to talk to break the awful quiet. "Well, thank goodness nobody's hurt. I wonder if the others heard the shot. Look, Sandy, you can hardly see where the bullet went in." I touched the place tentatively. "In fact...."

"Hmm," he said. He knew what I was thinking. In my mind, the truth was too terrible to tell. How could we say, "We shot a hole in the house?" How could we say that to the Fergusons?

"Well, let's get ready," Sandy said, as serious as I'd ever seen him.

Ready for what, I wondered, but didn't ask.

We made one more check around the no-longer-perfect Little House, straightening a dish cloth, blowing an ash back into the fireplace, avoiding the bedroom. Our tires crunched loudly on the gravel as we drove up the hill. Sandy parked behind Tinky's spotless truck. He and Aunt Nina had come back. Great.

I didn't want to get out of the car, and made an excuse of wiping a spot off Ruben's shirt. In contrast, Sandy purposefully entered the house and reemerged with Daddy, who was sipping from a coffee mug. Through the windshield, I watched the pantomime.

Sandy spoke briefly. Daddy's eyebrows went up, his mouth turned down. It was his disgusted look. I saw him say "What?" Sandy spoke again. Daddy shook his head and threw out his coffee. He pointed to himself and gestured toward the house. Sandy shook his head "no" and went back through the screen door. In a minute, he was back with Tinky, and I watched him tell the story again. Then the three men walked down the hill, Sandy between them like a prisoner.

I sat in the car facing forward until Ruben began to protest against being confined in the back seat. I unfastened his seat belt with sweaty hands. When I turned around, the men had reappeared and Tinky was patting Sandy on the back. Daddy was not quite smiling. They both knew what it had cost Sandy to come clean, to own up to an accident they might never have discovered, to expose himself to the Fergusons' scorn. I was witnessing the recognition and celebration of courage.

By the time the breakfast dishes had been washed, dried, and put away, the whole family knew what had gone on in the Little House. I heard Aunt Hayes say to Cousin Ben, "Well, even the big monkeys fall out of the tree sometimes." We were not going to be frozen out of the family. In fact, we had contributed, once again, to its anthology of stories.

But my joy was mixed with envy. I had spent my life believing that being a Ferguson was a full-time, all-consuming job, and Sandy was proving me wrong. He would never be burdened with my family's dark vision of cracks as crisis, dents as disaster. Yet when events required it, he could assume the Ferguson role, their desire for order and setting things right. He could have his cake and eat it too, and never mind the crumbs.

The Minner Olympics

Missy eyed my cousin's new bathing suit. "Carrie Mae, now that you're a young matron, don't you think all those pink ruffles are a tee-tiny bit girlish? Now, Marybeth there, with her cute little figure, could do that suit proud." Missy got two reactions. Marybeth, who knew she was being pity-flattered, smiled a bruised smile. Carrie said, "You're just trying to drag me down into crone-dom with you, Missy Bell. I'm not wearing brown and navy till I'm eighty."

Nowhere else had I heard women talk to one other like this and still be friends. Maybe it helped that they were all some kind of kin to each other—or their families had known each other for so long they might as well be. We had set up a village of beach chairs, umbrellas, blankets, and coolers at the high tide mark in front of the Bells' cottage—a misnomer, since the house had four bedrooms and an equal number of baths. These women and their husbands and children spent the summers on each others' decks and porches, meeting in twos and threes in the early mornings to walk briskly on the beach, again at 11:00 to enjoy the water before the sun turned up to broil, and again at 5 o'clock sharp for wine and shrimp and crab cakes.

It was a close, closed community. I was there because as Carrie's first cousin, I was granted temporary entry when I came to visit from the Midwest—a region in which none of these people had the slightest interest. Still, I liked them. Most of them. Most of the time. They were Carrie's friends (she was married-in, not blood kin) and I loved my cousin. And they were always generous with each other, smart about what interested them, funny—and completely, unapologetically, and infallibly themselves.

When Marybeth, in her white crocheted bikini, walked down to the waves to "get wet," (nobody in this crowd actually *swam* in the ocean) Missy's older sister and next-door neighbor Cora said, "Hasn't it been almost two months since her little dooie? Careful now, or the children will hear." As she put her finger to her lips, her gold bracelets flashed in the sun. Ten-year-old Ross Bell and Cora's similarly-aged and dramatically bored daughter Leighton were making drip castles nearby with Carrie's four-year-old Lilly.

"Well, you ought to know," Missy said. "You were the one who rescued her from that nasty police station, and drove her to her AA meetings."

"And you were the one who took care of those precious, terrible twins while she did community service, putting bows on funeral arrangements at Miss Ella's flower shop."

I will never belong to a group of people so completely as these people belong to each other, I thought. And, briefly, that made me sad.

"Y'all hush now," Carrie said, "She's coming. Here, Marybeth, honey, I stole your chair. You can have it back. And that is a mighty cute suit."

"Bring that chair over here by me, pretty girl," Skipper Bell told her. "I have a present for you," and he handed her a bottle of water from the cooler. Missy's husband was long and languid. In his spare time, he was a lawyer in nearby Elizabeth City, a fact he never mentioned. At the beach, he was an excellent host, a daddy to his and Missy's son Ross (Missy and Cora's maiden name), and a fisherman. In fact, it was rare for any of the men to sit on the beach with the womenfolk. They were usually out on the ocean or Pamlico Sound in their powerful, sleek boats, catching blues and mackerel to bring home for supper. Indeed, Carrie's husband Paul and my Sandy were even now engaged in that activity. Skipper, Marybeth's bulky, perpetually sunburned husband Walter Allen, and brown, bald Tommy, who belonged to Cora, had been enticed to sit with us by the promise of a Blicker.

I'd been present three summers ago at the first Blicker, a combination of brunch and liquor served on the beach. Remembering the hilarity, I looked forward, with reservation, to this one. While I nursed my own second drink—and my sense of separateness—I'd made a study of watching the different effects of alcohol before noon on the beach crowd. My cousin Carrie found everything beautiful: "Y'all just look at that white gull against that blue sky. After my nap, I'm going to paint that." Marybeth got loud, Cora got quiet, Skipper, who always drank moderately, smiled. Walter Allen and Tommy, decent men as a rule, lost, in Skipper's words, "two-thirds of their manners." They took turns picking at Marybeth until she had moved from laughter to anger, or tears. Wisely, they never teased Cora or Missy.

"Here comes Mason to join us," Missy said. "He must have just finished his workout." Of the admirably-muscled figure walking toward us, Ross said, "Remember when he was fat?"

"Oh child," said Cora, "I remember when he was a sad, pudgy little boy. His daddy, Cousin Warren Marshall, was a hard-hunting, hard-drinking man. He brought Mason to school and made him tell the class he had to repeat first grade. Poor Mason was blubbering to beat all."

The men seldom contributed to the women's combination of gossip and history, but Tommy added, "He cried again on the opening day of deer season—he must have been about nine—when Mr. Warren made him shoot that little buck and then blooded him. That boy couldn't decide whether to beller or throw up. Shamed his daddy that day for sure."

"I didn't cry when you blooded me, did I, Daddy?" Ross asked. "I was tough."

"Yes, you were, but that's not something we brag about, is it," said Skipper, putting his hand on his son's blonde head. He went on, "It's a fact that Mason Spencer wasn't born with a tub of testosterone, but he's made something pretty out of what he got. And here he is now. Have a chair, Mason, if you're through torturing yourself on that weight machine."

Mason, bronze of chest and white of teeth, assumed a yoga position in the sand next to Missy. "Glad to see all of you," he said, "but given the choice between conversing with the manly men or the luscious ladies, I choose the latter. Has the Blicker started?"

"Just waiting for you, my friend," Skipper told him. "I do think a little drink would be most welcome about now."

Missy and Cora stood, brushed at their sandy bottoms, and headed toward the Bells' house, running the last few feet through the hot sand. Cora called back, "Come on, Leighton. You can make the shrimp sauce," and her daughter scrambled up, eager to join the adults.

In fifteen minutes, they were back, Cora carrying a bag of ice, a stack of plastic cups and a handful of straws. Leighton had the shrimp and the secret family sauce. Missy was holding a bright pink plastic trash can against her chest, walking carefully because it was full of very strong daiquiris.

"Sweet libation," said Mason, and soon everyone was sipping a cold drink, including Ross and Leighton, who were encouraged to try a little 'to see how it makes you feel.' When Lilly pouted, Carrie gave her a swallow from her cup.

Half an hour later, the trash can was all but empty. Missy handed out the straws, saying, "Gather round, now. We all know the rum sinks to the bottom," and in a kind of communion, we drank the potent dregs. Skipper rescued two straws, folding them back and forth, back and forth, into inch worms for the children.

Tommy and Ben Allen, who had been whispering together, made their slightly wobbly way to Cora's cottage. When they reappeared, they were wearing black Lone Ranger masks and bandanas over their noses. Tommy had stuck a cap pistol in the elastic waist of his bathing suit. A delighted Leighton shouted, "Mamma, they found the cowboy stuff from last Halloween." Sputtering with laughter, the two men explained that they were going down the beach to Walter Allen and Marybeth's house to pay a surprise visit to Grace Ann, the twins' 14-year-old nanny for the summer.

"We won't scare her bad," Tommy said. "We just want her to have a story to tell when she gets home."

Marybeth said, "Don't you wake up those babies," and sat back with her empty cup.

"If we do, we'll roll them in sand and bring them back to their loving mamma," her husband told her.

Somebody in this crowd should stop them, I thought, but no one did. I looked at Carrie, who shook her head and shrugged. Then, a guilty bystander, I stood and watched them go.

When the two men had galloped their imaginary horses down the beach, Skipper said quietly to his wife, "You know Grace Ann is granddaughter to old Ron Wiggins, who makes a living taking rich Yankees bear hunting. I expect that girl has a skinning knife in her purse. A little phone call might save us all a mess of trouble."

Missy was moving toward the house before he finished speaking. When she came back, she gave her husband's arm a quick pat, and Skipper unfolded himself from the beach chair. It was clear that he'd had enough of the Blicker and meant to shift our gathering to a higher plane. "Get up, y'all," he said. "The Blicker's over and now we're gonna wash our sins away. It's time for the Minner Olympics. Here's what you do first. Yes, you, too, Marybeth darlin'. Find yourself a stick—can be a stalk of sea oats—and break it into little pieces. Might as well get some for our merry pranksters, I reckon. Come here, sweet child," he said to Lilly. "Uncle Skipper will show you how." And every one of us—the very young, the slurred of speech, the unsure of foot—rose to do Skipper's bidding.

Walter Allen and Tommy reappeared, wiping their red faces with the bandanas. "Whoa Nellie," said Tommy, "that Grace Ann should be a Marine. She met us at the door with blood in her eye and a can of pepper spray in her hand. We couldn't snatch those masks off fast enough."

Walter Allen chimed in. "Then she told us she knew it was us all along. She just wanted to prove how safe she was keeping those twins. Wonder how she recognized us?"

"You boys just can't hide your masculine charms," Skipper said. "Too bad. It was such a clever scheme." Skipper's tone was nothing like the soft bantering the women used to insult each other.

The two men exchanged surprised looks, but before they could grope their way to anger, Skipper had put them to work breaking sea oat stalks into two-inch lengths, and soon they were part of the current project.

When he saw everyone was ready, Skipper scooped up Lilly and moved toward the ocean as if he were walking down a church aisle. And we all followed our leader, holding our little sticks.

Ordinarily, I entered the ocean slowly, by increments, giving feet, thighs, and waist time to adjust to the always-chilly Atlantic. Skipper, however, walked into the surf at the same pace he had crossed the sand, the determination of his going out an evident match for the tide's coming in. Soon, we were out beyond the breakers, the shortest of us up to our necks in a sea that gently rose and fell.

"All right, dear ones, now is the time to cast your sticks upon the waters." Like everyone else, I obeyed.

For the space of one wave, nothing happened. And then, a minnow, three minnows, tiny flashes in the sun, emerged from the ocean and jumped over the sticks. Then there were a hundred, united members of their own community. Then there were none. Amazement kept us quiet. How brief. How beautiful. Skipper announced, "Ladies and gentlemen, you have borne witness to the Minner Olympics," and we applauded the man responsible for our pleasure. Delighted with each other and slightly tipsy, we went home for a nap in our sandy-sheeted beds.

Cowboys

Growing up with Holden Caulfield has put me on a permanent lookout for phonies. So I was cautious in my enthusiasm when Sandy said, "Let's go out to Larry Brannian's ranch in Wyoming when we're both through teaching in May." I remembered Larry from our first year in Grinnell when we were scouting for farmland. He was a dark-haired, fit auctioneer who had done some rodeoing in central Iowa. He had laughed at me once when Pascal, my big bay quarter horse, had one of his bucking spells. But I had enjoyed Larry's lively auctioneer patter at the sales where Sandy and I checked out the horses, and I'd admired the white Stetson he always wore for his performances. Most Iowans are as phony-alert as I am, and I gave Larry credit for the courage to fly that Stetson cowboy banner amongst all those sober feed caps. But what, I wondered, had he made of himself in Wyoming since he moved his family there fifteen years ago? Would he wear angora chaps and shirts with fringe? Was Sandy taking me to a dude ranch?

That Larry had made a video promoting his UM ranch and hunting lodge—and that he had posted it online, where it appeared when I looked him up—did not reassure me. The film showed beautiful country, all right, and horses (my chief interest), but it also included a video of a group of people sitting rather awkwardly around a campfire while a fellow with a cowboy hat and guitar sang western songs. I didn't watch it all.

By late May, though, arrangements had been made, and I told friends that we were going out west for our annual cowboy fix. If any of them were inclined to be amused at a couple of academics playing cowboy, I wanted to beat them to the draw. During the long and pleasant drive to Wyoming, I had time to fret first about whether our experience would be real, and then about whether it would be too real. I imagined myself on a strange horse, teetering on a six-inch trail with a sheer mountain face going straight up on one side and straight down on the other. Then I thought about Larry Brannian laughing when my horse bucked.

The UM ranch is just outside Buffalo, Wyoming, a small town of 1,500 with a small, decent-looking museum—good— three antique stores, and one place that sells "authentic Indian replicas"—not good. The signs continued to be mixed as we drove the last stretch to the ranch. We passed through a cluster of "ranchettes," the varnish on the very new log houses glowing gold under the sun. But the toy spreads disappeared, the road narrowed to tar and gravel, and we could see the snow-topped Big Horns in the not-too-distant distance.

As we neared the Brannians' place, I tried to decide what I was so anxious to see. A handsome building like the Cartwright home on *Bonanza* with tree trunks for porch columns wouldn't do—too careful, too copied. But a little brick home with petunias in cement urns would really disappoint me. And there it was—a low house with dark red siding set down in a clump of cottonwoods. The house could have used—what?—antlers over the door? A horse hitched out front? I wasn't sure what I wanted. Further down the driveway, the big barn and horse trailer were reassuring, as were the sort-of border collies who met and then lost interest in us.

Larry was soon at the door, welcoming and waving us in. I liked the way he looked. His brown and smooth-cheeked face was textured by deep lines at the corners of blue eyes that matched the blue and white check of his western shirt. He stood there sock footed, and his blue denim jeans were somehow neither new nor old. Had he worked toward that effect, I wondered. Had all that blue come together by accident?

He gave us coffee at the kitchen table—put my milk in a little pitcher—and suggested we visit just a bit before loading up. I considered the word "visit." Did cowboys visit? But our talk was easy and informative. Larry described the UM ranch: 4,000 acres of grazing land and 40,000 more of allotment in the national forest; 300 head of cattle; his horses, some for working cows, some for breeding. He still auctioneered for livestock and antique sales. He hadn't rodeoed in a while. Had tried it again a couple of years ago, but a saddle bronc had thrown him and stuck his head in the ground.

With the second cup of coffee, he started telling stories. One was about coming out to Wyoming for the first time one December, because a friend had said they could get rich trapping coyotes. So he and this friend lived in a cave for a month and kept track of the days by making notches on a stick. They lost count of the notches, but left on what they thought was the day the friend's wife was to pick them up. Fighting their way through a terrific blizzard, they came out on the highway exactly where her car was parked. She'd been waiting for five minutes. They made ten dollars off the coyote skins. Good story.

The next one was bigger. For three years running, until the liability got too high, he had organized a Wild West show in Buffalo. It had everything: roping, horse and bull riding, and Indians. Indians who drove him crazy because they had their own notion of time and refused to be controlled by the clock, arriving hours, sometimes days late. Indians who wore ball caps and tee shirts instead of the beads and feathers he'd requested. One year, he'd booked two spectacular acts—a sharpshooter who could throw a knife then draw and fire his pistol, and the knife would stick right in the hole the bullet made, and a courageous young man from the Sioux tribe whose specialty was riding a bucking buffalo. He'd given that Indian top billing—called him Willy Everride—and everybody wanted to see his act.

When Willy didn't appear, Larry gave the crowd their money's worth by putting on a long black wig he just happened to have handy, plus his leather fringed britches, and riding the buffalo himself. Even his wife, Eva, didn't recognize him—until his wig fell off in mid-buck and he was exposed as an impostor. The audience loved the whole thing, including the impostor bit, and I wondered if there ever had been a buffalo-riding Indian at all.

Just as my This-is-fun-but-are-we-wasting-time-here alarm was about to go off, Larry slapped his thighs, said, "We'd better get rolling. Two days in the mountains are gonna go fast," and went to find his boots—gray and blue, they matched the eyes and the shirt and the jeans. On his way out the door, he took a hat off a peg and settled it on his head. It had been white once, and still was in places. The hat-band, snaggle-toothed bead work, blue and pink and cream, had been loosely and inexpertly stitched in place. Had he bought it that way? I fought down covetousness and envy: if I had such a hat, I'd have to wear it in the bathroom. No occasion in my life would allow me to appear in such a revealing disguise.

To me, he said, "This won't take long." To Sandy, he said, "Come on, you can see the barn." I nosed around the house, which was perfectly neat and obviously loved—Eva, I suspected. The furniture was a combination of new and modest, old and handsome. But I wanted to see the horses being loaded, and I'd started out the door when I noticed a shelf of books in this otherwise un-bookish house. All Will James. And I was nine again, reading *Smoky the Cow Horse* for the third or fourth time, dimly aware that my mother hoped I'd put down the book and go outside to play with the other kids.

I got to the barn just in time to see the last two horses—a big, serviceable sorrel and a gorgeous little paint stallion, black and white—walk into the trailer. I heard Larry call the paint Gizmo. Would one of them be mine? Was I hoping for beauty or duty?

The preparations were completely without the frenzy I associated with loading horses. The ones in the trailer stood quiet; the ones loading went in without being led, as if approaching a full hayrack. Through the slats, I saw a palomino hindquarter and a docile bay face with a wide white blaze. Larry pulled the big rig up to the house and we loaded our stuff.

Should I wear my boots? I asked him, anxious for him to see they weren't new.

"Probably."

Should I bring my down jacket?

"Could, might."

We brought out the plastic sacks of groceries from the house. A cat snatched a piece of string cheese from the one I'd set on the ground, and Larry said, "That was your share," but he smiled. Then he addressed the dogs, and his voice changed. I'd call it baby talk, except none of the words were silly. Just the pitch and inflections made him sound like he was talking to grandchildren: "Want to go, guys? Well, get on, then." Blackie and Patches assumed their traveling positions on the truck bed—legs stiff, noses up and forward—and we were away. Only the truck seemed reluctant, growling and coughing as it dragged its heavy load toward the mountains.

We pulled off at the entrance to French Creek Road, which rolled upward through larkspur and lupine, pine and aspen. I recognized the beauty, but I couldn't concentrate on it. The big question had my full attention: which horse would I ride? I wasn't sure I had a choice, but between the ranch and French Creek, caution had defeated romance and pride, and I said I'd be glad for a gentle one. I rode, I assured Larry, but I didn't enjoy being afraid. "I won't scare you, Betty," Larry said, and I believed him, and silently rejoiced. "You'll be riding Chester. We don't want to call him old, but he's steady and seasoned." Chester was the blaze-faced bay I'd seen through the slats. Two minutes ground-tied in the sun, and his eyes were half-closed, his bottom lip slack. A broke-to-death horse for the lady rider. But he was tall and glossy, and he perked up as I swung my leg across the saddle. Sandy was to ride the sorrel, Red—a plain name, but a cut above Chester—Larry would be on Trigger, alternately known as Yaller, and the glorious Gizmo was the pack horse.

When I asked Larry, partly as a joke, if he thought the little stud felt insulted, he treated my comment as an honest question: "Well, I don't know, but it's a good way to train a three-year-old. He learns to be humble, and those salt blocks he's carrying will punch him in the sides if he brushes up against a tree. That way, he'll steer clear of tree trunks when he's carrying a rider." Gizmo's pack-saddle, a neat construction of wood and canvas, bulged with the salt, our sleeping bags, and food, and Larry apologized for the whatever-works way he was passing the rope around the bulges.

"So," said I, trying again for banter, "the diamond hitch I always read about in my cowboy books is just a fiction."

"No," he answered quickly, a little sharply. "There's a perfect diamond on Gizmo's other side. I'm just trying to save time, and I may be sorry for it."

Larry left the truck key on the top of the right trailer tire, under the fender, explaining that all the ranchers left their keys in the same place, in case somebody needed to move—or use—a vehicle. Then, with the same absence of flurry I'd appreciated before, our little pack train was off, Larry first, leading Gizmo, Sandy and I switching off third and fourth positions. The seasoned Chester must have been a lead horse at some time during his long life on the trail, because that's the place he really wanted. He was realistic, grudgingly acknowledging Yaller's dominance as the younger, faster horse, but he would not willingly be done out of third place by his old friend Red. So began a subtle, quiet conflict between Chester and me that lasted throughout the trip:

142

I wanted him to be content and relaxed—but stylish—wherever he was in line; he wanted the honor due him as senior horse. This struggle perhaps kept us from forming that bond I still hope for from early exposure to Walter Farley's *Black Stallion* stories, but I learned to respect Chester, and riding through the Big Horns on his high, wide back, I was never afraid.

I "might could" have needed my down jacket, but I didn't. It had snowed in Buffalo the week before and the mountains had fresh caps, but the air was now sweet and bright, warm in the open and cool in the trees. That first afternoon, I argued quietly with Chester, got used to being thrown against the cantle of the saddle on the inclines and against the horn on the declines, watched Blackie's and Patches' joy in the pursuit of marmots, more colorfully known as rock chucks or whistle pigs, and studied Larry's alternate gentleness and severity with Yaller and Gizmo.

Yaller was really his grandson's horse, and Larry was discouraging any tendencies to buck or bolt, making him a safe mount for the young boy—if "safe" can be applied to a horse. He praised the palomino when he stepped readily into a fast stream or moved steadily through a boggy patch. (Chester hated the bogs and clambered through as if some terrible force sucked at his hooves.) But if Yaller (the name was subversive; the horse was beautiful—perfectly shaped, with long cream mane and tail) shied or bolted, he was punished. There were no spurs or quirt; Larry just powered him, with knees and seat and reins, back into correctness.

Gizmo he treated with special affection, as if to make up for his role as pack-animal. His hand was often on the horse's neck and he addressed him in the same kind of tickling voice he had used with the dogs. But I saw him twice react to Gizmo's breach of conduct with a quick, hard jerk on the halter—no yelling, no hitting—just a swift reminder of the order of things.

We talked some as we rode: here was a good spot to look for elk antler sheds, there were mule deer droppings, there the graceful clown herself; here were beer cans and plastic sacks, the droppings of the elk hunters who came in on RVs. Bow hunters, backpackers, and trail riders, Larry told us, were generally clean; the motorized elk hunters were "filthy." I resolved not to be filthy.

Along about evening, we opened and rode through a wire gate into a grove of straight silver aspens, and there was the cabin. It was right. Old logs, recently re-chinked, a plank porch with two-by-four railings. What should we do with the horses?

"Oh, close the gate and let them go. There's plenty of grass and the stream's high. Hear it? That's where we'll cool the drinks. Just put the bottles in a sack and tie it to a low branch." I knew the procedure. I had even used it long ago in a private cowboy scenario, though my sack broke and most of the bottles got away. I was glad I didn't have to be amazed. I looked at the grazing horses among the ruler-straight aspens. I looked at the smiling, panting dogs lying on the porch. I breathed deep and was happy.

"Come on in."

Two rooms. The front was the kitchen. In the center was a handsome wood-burning cookstove with bright chrome trim.

"Where'd you get this?" I asked.

"Didn't. It was here when I started using the place. Cooks good."

On the kitchen table was a penciled note:

Larry,

I spent a night on the way to Rock Creek. Ate a can of your chili so I owe you. See you in town.

Dave

The back room had narrow cots with rusty springs and a thick bundle of foam pad hanging from a rafter. I knew that trick too. The pad was supposed to be out of reach of mice or other rodents who might fancy foam. But some clever animal had found a way to navigate the rafter and rope because chunks had been chewed off the edge of the dangling pad. The cots were close together, and there were three of them.

"You take the bed by the window, Betty. It has a mattress." So it did. I wondered what had been sleeping on it. The window had a red-checked curtain and a sill full of flies, living and dead. Larry opened it, and the live ones left.

"And Sandy, you can use the foam pad."

What will you do?

"Oh, I always sleep out on the ground. I'm glad for the fresh air."

Did he mean directly on the ground? Would he use a saddle for a pillow? All night or just long enough for us to witness it? Regardless, I was glad for the privacy.

"How about some supper?"

Yes! And the hot dogs and string cheese I had regarded with tolerance at the ranch took on new meaning.

Could I help?

"Nope, you're on vacation, and I'm used to cooking up here."

And with the same absence of visible effort I had noted at the horse loading, the hot dogs were cooking over a campfire, a can of pork and beans was bubbling, and a bag of salad had been produced, with three kinds of dressing.

"See, this is the cowboy way for beans," Larry said, and pulling on a soft leather glove, he lifted the steaming can by its bent-back lid, inserted a spoon, and offered the beans around.

"I found this glove. It's a real nice one. Some New York lady staying at Paradise Ranch probably dropped it." Paradise, I knew, was a local, very expensive dude ranch. I imagined the woman of the missing glove in stiff new jeans and stiff new wide-brimmed hat, red silk shirt, and Gore-Tex cowboy boots. I smoothed my sweatshirt with a satisfied smile.

Wonderful hot dogs. Wonderful beans. Wonderful bottle of white wine we had brought from Iowa, chilled in the stream, and opened after dinner. Larry accepted a small cup of wine and then talked briefly about some ugly drinking he had witnessed among his friends. "Seeing what it did to some of my buddies, I've never had much use for it," and he didn't finish even his short portion. To change the subject, I said, "I saw the Will James collection at your house. Are you a fan?"

"He's my hero." I understood that he was dead serious about the author, and was glad to say "Oh, he was mine, too." The different tenses were significant. I meant that I had loved *Smoky the Cowhorse* and a couple of other books whose titles I've lost, and that I'd looked for signs that my pony, Slicker, would be as loyal to me as Smoky was to his cowboy owner. Larry meant, I soon realized, that Will James, the man, had been and still was a model for him.

"I don't read much. Don't have time. But I've read everything Will James wrote. He was a real cowboy. He could do it all—rope, ride, nurse cattle. He bought a ranch in Montana and was doing well with it until the Hollywood crowd who was making movies of his stuff ruined him—or he ruined himself. He couldn't deal with all that put-on-glamour way of life. He died in Hollywood. That's a shame."

We talked about something else for a while—hunting antelope, his nine young grandchildren (I remember three of their names: Dakota, Cheyenne, and Chance)—and then he said, "You know, he taught himself to be a cowboy. Will James wasn't his real name. He made it up because his real name, Beaupre, didn't sound Western. I guess he kind of created himself, like he did his stories."

I thought, *Pay attention here. You're about to learn something.* But my delighted senses were too busy for insights, and, slightly high on wine, woodsmoke, and the proximity of horses, I was pleased to be distracted by Blackie, the smaller and shyer of the two dogs, who was sidling up to me with a "Would-petting-be-possible?" twist of her head. I reached out to oblige, but Larry saw Blackie's overture as begging, and he didn't allow his dogs to beg.

"Off the porch, Blackie," he said, and Blackie turned to go. Then Larry said, "Oh, sorry Blackie," and to me, "She's bringing you something. She does that to people she likes." Blackie came forward, placed a small pine cone in my palm, sat for a brief ear scratching, and left the porch again. Gratified beyond reason, I stood up. It was bedtime.

Love this

But I stayed a few moments to watch Larry's preparations. He unfurled his bedroll, a heavy canvas-covered affair, on a level stretch of ground about ten yards from the campfire. "See, this is what the cowboys use." Again, I wondered about verb tense. Had he said "use" or "used"? Was this how cowboys slept now, or was this bag and practice a reproduction? His bedroll was clearly something more than a thin Indian blanket, which is what the cowboys of young adult fiction and Saturday matinees slept under. Picking up the bedroll and unscrolling it with a clatter, he demonstrated that it was literally a bag, into which he had dropped a coffee pot, skillet, pliers, jacket, and spare reins. Then he pulled off his boots, said goodnight, and disappeared inside it—my cue that the show was over.

Two, three, or maybe four hours later, I woke up still happy but aware of a very full bladder. The "shitter," as Larry had unapologetically called it, was a long way off, and I'd have to pass over or around Larry to get to it. The night was chilly, the ground wet from recent snow, and I had gone to bed in my sweatshirt and socks, with nothing in between, to air some budding saddle sores. But I was sleepy and still buzzy enough from the wine to make going outside in that attire seem appropriate. No problem with light; the moon gave the aspens long straight shadows.

I made my way soundlessly, I thought, to the porch steps. Then a dog barked, a quick sharp series—Patches, I'm sure, not my friend Blackie—and there I was, on a stage, lit up and bottomless, saying, "It's all right, it's ok, it's just me," and watching Larry's bedroll for movement. The dog quieted and I made my way around the far side of the cabin, where I accomplished my mission, soaked my socks (on the wet ground), took in the silver-gray of the moonlight and some sounds I liked but couldn't identify, and beat it back to my bed, only glancing at the pale rectangle of the cowboy bedroll for fear I'd see a pair of open eyes.

When daylight came, I was rested and ready. The ointment I had known to bring along to put on my saddle sores had helped, and my socks had nearly dried in the warmth of my sleeping bag. I liked climbing back into yesterday's jeans—and when I stepped out on the porch, Larry's easy "Good morning" suggested he hadn't seen my fashion show, or wasn't letting on. The horses had been saddled, a small fire made, and eggs with onions, ham, and green peppers were ready for the frying pan.

Over breakfast, Larry asked, "You hear the coyotes last night?"

"Oh, is that what they were," I said, remembering the noises in the night. I wished I'd listened more carefully. Coyotes howled in the book of every Western author I'd ever read, from Zane Grey to Cormac McCarthy.

"Yeah. Gizmo came and stood right over me."

He's going to say Gizmo was protecting him, I thought. He's going to make that claim.

"Yeah, he stood right over my head. He was scared, I guess. And I was scared he was going to jump and step on my face, so we were a couple of wakeful fellows there for a bit."

Even if it meant Larry and Gizmo had witnessed my bareness in the moonlight, I loved this honest picture of horse and master.

In fact, I loved almost all of that day. Our object was to take the salt blocks up to the highest meadows so the cows would be enticed up to the hills, giving the lower pastures some relief from over-grazing. It was a logical and effective plan. It also allowed

149

Sandy and me to believe we were helping, or at least observing and learning, instead of being catered to. Along the way, we saw antelope and mule deer, and—Larry signaled "quiet" and then "look there"—two elk crossing into the woods ahead of us. We rode through country whose beauty tightened my breathing, and we stopped once to rest in a wide cup of grasses and flowers, bordered on one side with rock columns and chimneys and on the other with dark green forest.

When the pack saddle was empty, Larry took off Gizmo's lead, and the little horse behaved like a happy child, tearing off down the mountain and then stopping to look back: "Coming?" If our way was different, he'd pretend not to care; he'd snatch a few mouthfuls of grass, then amble and then bound back to us, his pleasure in his freedom countered by his instinct to herd.

Twice Larry acknowledged danger. Once when the trail became suddenly steep, narrow, and rocky, he said, "I'd advise getting off here and walking down. It'd be easier on the horses— and on us if one of them slipped and somersaulted down. Sandy, you lead Red but stay to the side of him"—tricky on that slender path. "I'll take Yaller and Chester, and, Betty, you come down on your own." It was a clear though gently-phrased concession to the lady, and I thought of protesting…before I considered the slope of the trail, my slick and high-heeled cowboy boots, and reason. I said, "OK" and then I slipped and clattered to the bottom.

As I remounted, Larry said without a bit of irony, "You know, sometimes it's good to get off just to stretch your legs. We've been in the saddle quite a while. So, Betty, you just say when you'd like to stop."

I'd have died first.

The second difficulty came at a stream which, though easily fordable in normal weather, was now a crashing, foaming flood. The horses, who had heard its roil long before we could, approached tensely. Larry pulled Yaller up and clipped the lead back on Gizmo, who had crowded against the palomino's rump. He studied the water for a while, and then turned in the saddle to consult us. It was hard to speak above the flood's static, so he looked his question. I tried to make my expression say, "Looks bad, but I'm game." I didn't want to cross that water.

I'd just finished rereading Faulkner's *As I Lay Dying*, and the image of the drowned and bloated mules caught in the flood was strong. But I believed in Larry's promise not to scare me, and I wasn't afraid. So along with relief came a thread of disappointment when Larry shook his head and turned his horse.

When we could hear words again, he said, "I don't know. Maybe we could've. But it would have been risky." Then he said two things I liked him for. The first was, "*Maybe* I would have tried it if I'd been by myself." (I liked the presence of and emphasis on "Maybe.") The second was, "We didn't want to take a chance of breaking a horse's leg on those rolling rocks." He could have said, "We didn't want to take a chance with a woman along." Maybe he meant that, but he didn't say it.

"Well, that means I won't get to show you Dusty's cabin. He's the old guy who was a kind of hermit writer, who got sick and died up here because he didn't want to come down among people again. But there're two other ways back, both good trails. One goes up through Paradise Ranch, the other doubles back the way we came and is quite a bit longer. If we go that way, we'll be riding four or five more hours. I'll let you folks decide."

It was clear that we were supposed to choose the shorter way, but I wasn't ready to be among people either. My saddle sores were stinging and my knees ached. My knees, for heaven's sake. No book had ever mentioned cowboys having bad knees. But I didn't want what we'd been doing, and being, to end. Larry leaned on us a little. "You know, if we go the long way, it'll be near dark when we get back to the trailer, and I want you to see my stud and brood mare this evening. Besides, I don't know about you, but Larry Brannian has had about enough of the saddle for one day."

I think that was his gracious way of saying I know you're not soft, not quitters. But maybe he was worried he'd never get us off his horses and we'd be on the trail forever, Ghost Riders in the Sky.

Eventually, we saw Paradise Ranch, saw the glowing, scrubbed, crowded-together cabins, small copies of those on the ranchettes, saw the long, slow lines of carefully casual people on nose-to-tail horses, being led by their carefully "Cowboy" guide through this "Authentic Western Ranch." Sandy and I exchanged a glance. We were glad not to be part of this scene, glad not to be dudes, me in my sweatshirt, he in his ball cap. We were proud of our status as real…well, real what? I wondered. Real teachers? That designation sure lacked fire or flare.

Larry and two of the guides stopped awhile and had a friendly chat. Gizmo's manners were perfect—better than Sandy's and mine. He never once announced his manhood, his superiority to those winding strings of horses. Pretty soon, we were past the ranch and climbing again, one last time before the end of the trail.

The end, like the beginning, was smooth and quick.

Should I loosen Chester's girth before he gets in the trailer?

"Could. Do what you want to." Pause. "I do," Larry said with a smile. He lifted the satisfied, exhausted Patches into the truck bed—Blackie had managed on her own—put his face close to the dogs' muzzles, said some more of those sweet-toned words, closed the trailer's tailgate, and we were off.

Down off the mountain, out of the big spaces we'd been riding through, I became aware of Larry's push and energy, and how he was moving our little group through the rest of the agenda. Back at the ranch (I savored the phrase) Larry said to me, "We'll unload. I know you'll want a shower." In fact, I didn't, much. I was proud of the dirt I'd acquired, of the beginning of slickness on the inside of my clothes, and I was reluctant to lose it, but it's hard to refuse an order that's phrased like a favor, so I started toward the house. Eva, a trim, pretty blonde woman with a soft voice, came out to say hello. I wondered about the balance between her and her husband. Was he the battery, the force, and she the softening insulation? He had spoken of her with pride—in her looks, her good job at the bank. How did cowboys treat their wives?

The men were back from the barn before I was out of the shower. Larry and I crossed paths and nodded as he headed for his turn in the bathroom. His wooly torso seemed to take up all the space in the narrow hall. Minutes later, still wet, he was searching on his hands and knees, calling, "Eva, where's that tape?" He found it under the TV. "We don't watch television, can't get reception out here, but we've got stacks of tapes. The grandkids stick them anywhere." Soon Sandy and I were watching a documentary on Will James, the French Canadian who made himself into a real cowboy and then drowned in alcohol and fiction.

In the kitchen, Larry was on the phone—to the Buffalo auctioneer—a man in Kansas, he'd explained later, who wanted a hunt in the fall, to his grandson—laughing, doing business, catching up.

Dinner was good—meatloaf cooked on the grill, hard rolls, a surprising salad with toasted peanuts. Larry said, "This is my favorite salad. I eat a lot of salad." I thought, *Cowboys and salads?* And we drank lemonade and tea. No beer, no wine. No sign of it, no offer made. He had accepted that small drink of wine at the cabin to give us permission to enjoy it ourselves.

Maybe, I thought, *all of this is invented for our pleasure, even the stories. Especially the stories.* As we ate, Larry entertained us by describing a Marlboro commercial that had been shot near Buffalo. "There's one guy—you'd recognize him—who's been in those commercials for thirty years. He and all those fellows are really good cowboys, every one of them. The director would say, 'Now, I want that yellow horse out front, with the white one ahead and the dark one behind.' And those guys would cut those horses to go just like that, at a full run. You can't do that unless you're good. And they were all friendly."

"We sat around with them between shots, me and some other guys from here who were supplying some extra horses. The older guy has lung cancer, but he just keeps on. He's adopted sixteen kids. And then the people who were doing the filming asked me if I'd like to try out for a commercial. They thought I might do, since I could ride and all, and they said I looked about right—

except my nose and chin were too close together. So, I said ok, why not, and they gave me a little block of wood to hold between my back teeth, but I guess that didn't do it, because I had a kind of screen test and all, but they didn't use me. That was ok. I was glad to know those guys."

A little later, with coffee steaming in front of us, Larry said, "The way I decided to come to Wyoming was a friend of mine told me we could get rich trapping coyotes out here."

I thought, "Hey, that's the trapping story. He's done this one before," and I was disappointed because I figured it must be a set piece he told to all the people he took up in the mountains and he'd forgotten he'd already done it for us. But this time he said, "We lived in a cave for about a week, but it was filthy, man. We were walking around in bat guano all the time, stumbling over carcasses some animals had drug in. So, after a few days, we made a kind of igloo. It was December and the snow was pretty deep. Well, it was cold, but it was clean. And then we ran across an old trapper's cabin and moved into it for the rest of the time. It was about halfway between the cave and the igloo as far as clean goes, but it was more like a house."

Was this the authentic version, then, I wondered. *Why had Larry been in the cave the whole time in the first telling? Did he alter the story to fit the occasion, his audience, his fancy? Or was this the complete edition, told to replace the earlier, abbreviated one?* I had no complaint about shaping facts to improve a story, but somehow this shift in detail shook awake my former concerns about phoniness.

Then it was time to move again. Larry said, "Come on. I want you to see those horses." As he spoke, he cleared and stacked our dirty dishes, and said to Eva, "I'll do these when we come back." I knew she'd wash them while we were gone, and so did he, but it was a decent offer.

The three of us rode in a small white pickup, which had a more delicate case of the same cough the big truck had. We drove past the house where his daughter and her family lived, past the site where, in the fall, Larry and Eva would begin to build their new place, and pulled up in the drive beside a blue-gray prefab.

"Want you to see my hunting lodge," Larry said, "where I put up the guys who come up for antelope and elk." And he propelled us into a handsome and spotless interior: across thick, powder-blue carpet, past the mounted heads of a "good" whitetail and a mule deer, through a bedroom with tight-sheeted bunks, and into a dustless kitchen.

Eva again, I thought, but I was sure this lodge must be the joint creation of interior decorator and cook Eva and her very smart, business-minded husband, who together had anticipated what kind of comfort their imported hunters would expect after a long day as keen-eyed stalkers. Back in the trophy room, Larry pointed out a tanned and felt-backed skin stretched for display on the wall.

"Cougar," he said. "One of my rancher neighbors called me last winter and said a lion was after his stock, had killed two heifers. Asked me if I'd go after it. So I spent two days tracking that old girl in the snow. And finally got her, just before dark. Shot her in one of those long deep gullies and had to carry her out on my back. Friend of mine in town took this picture."

Larry was holding a framed photograph, about 8x11, that, for me, filled up the room. The man in the picture was wearing one of those long dusters favored by the James and Dalton gangs in the movies. His perfectly right hat with its loose-beaded band was well down on his head, and he held the barrel of a gun whose stock rested by his right boot. Around his shoulders was draped the carcass of a mountain lion. He stood in front of what was either a Wyoming winter sunset or a pink-and-blue backdrop for school pictures. The portrait was staged: Larry was striking a pose. And the effect was magnificent.

He said, "I call this 'The End of the Day.'" He said that twice, and then he hung the picture back in its place.

In the truck on the way to the horses, I thought, *He made it all up. He imagined a whole life. And then he walked into it and lived it. He's filling in the details as he goes along, so any embellishment or revision he wants to make, he can. "Do what you want to. I do." Isn't that what he'd said?*

We bumped and rattled down a corduroy road, through a metal gate, and up a path, Larry talking now as if he needed to finish something, tell us the whole round story before our time was up.

"Those are my cows. I have every one on the computer, and I record what kind of calf she drops, whether she's a good mama, what the calf weighs at three months. If her performance is poor two years in a row—I always give them a second chance—she's history. So, I have a current chart of every one of these babies. Well, at least, Grandma Eva does. To tell the truth, I can't even turn the computer on."

We stopped in a rolling, treeless pasture, and Larry said, "There they are." In the distance, we could see two small groups of horses.

"Aw, oats. I meant to bring a bag of oats. Well, maybe I can fool them in." He opened his car door and pulled a throw rug off the back of the driver's seat, ran around to our side and performed a pantomime, turning the rug into a sack of invisible oats that he was pouring out on the ground as an offering to the horses.

"Oats, horses. Hey, horses, oats," he called.

And they came. From the right, three paints: stallion, mare, and foal—fine quarter horses, interested but suspicious of Larry's magic act.

"This is Chief, Gizmo's daddy. He's gentler than Chester. The grandkids ride him," he said of the splashy stud, whose jaws were as round and solid as skillets. "And this is my good brood mare." The mama put herself between us and her baby, sure now that Larry had fooled them. "And this little feller...." But now the horses from the left were arriving, and the ground shook. Four black Percherons, the spit and image of my uncle's horse, Dan, eager, expectant, demanding. "We use them in the winter to pull the hay wagons," Larry explained.

I'd stayed in the truck cab, thinking strangers might spook the horses, but these newcomers were anything but shy. A log-sized head came through the only open window, licked the steering wheel for salt, and bit the foam seat cushion, clearly thinking, "Ok, no oats. I'll eat what's here." I said to myself, with absolute seriousness, *"This is nightmare material,"* and Larry dashed around the truck to call off these giants.

"Sorry guys, sorry I let you down," he said, stroking a neck, touching a huge nose. Then to us through the open window, "These big old things scare me. They don't mean harm, but they're careless. And they don't much like jokes."

And that was the end of it. I slept less in Eva's spotless guest room than I had in the cabin. Woke up to a fragrant breakfast and a sense of dénouement. Larry was cordial, but was already on to the next thing—cows to be moved, a horse auction that afternoon.

"Good-bye, good-bye."

"Thanks, it was—great...."

"You all come back!"

On the way home, I thought these things: *What's the difference between written fiction and lived fiction? If you live it, how do you get out of it, end a chapter, close the book? How much energy and courage does it take to live that something you've made up? To outlast the skeptics? To offer them a piece of your fantasy?*

And I wondered, *if you live in a fiction of your own making, must you give up irony, and is that a sacrifice? Irony had been noticeably absent in Larry. What would I do without the gauze of irony that protects me from commitment: "Oh, I've done some acting but can't call myself an actor. A writer? No, I write a little, that's all." Wouldn't I miss the irony that makes me accept all things and doubt all things at once, that makes me buy my cowboy boots secondhand?*

Back home in my sweet Iowa town, Merle the barber was giving me a much-needed haircut.

"Merle," I said,"did you ever know a man named Larry Brannian?"

"Sure," he answered. "Me and everybody else. He was a good guy. Lived hard, though. Drank a lot. Why? You know him?"

The Family

That August morning, I opened the door of the old farm house, still so new to me, on a yard full of people, all moving, motioning, and shouting around a couple of rusty machines. The scene reminded me of a pre-battle ritual, except that nobody seemed mad. The Holmburgs had come to cut our hay.

Across the road on the land Sandy and I had recently purchased, the clover and alfalfa had ripened and was ready for harvest. Two years before, we had moved to the Midwest from North Carolina because a small, respectable college had offered us jobs. Though we'd pulled up our Southern roots, we couldn't shed the notion that owning land meant status and success, and we were delighted with our ninety-nine acres. We'd populated our little paradise with two horses, three dogs, and four barn cats. But we lacked the hands, the machinery, and the knowledge to convert our crop across the road into the big round bales that rested like peaceful whales in our neighbors' fields. The Holmburgs had all these necessities, though their battered tractor and mower, like the ancient blue truck they'd parked under the maple trees, seemed to have come from the bronze age, and we were glad to have found them. One of Sandy's hunting buddies had recommended them as dependable hard workers. He'd added, "They may not be just what you'd expect. Some of them are…. Well, you'll see." We were certain we'd like the Holmburgs fine. Sandy and I had long since rejected the dusty feudalism of the South, and four semesters of teaching in a college that embraced little-d democracy with a bear hug had made us adamant egalitarians. Besides, we needed their help.

Determined not to be seen as a hobby farmer who hired his work done, Sandy had already donned his Mule brand gloves and become part of the milling crowd. I was pretty sure I didn't know enough to be useful—a state which suited me very well—but I did want to be neighborly, and to check out this mysterious family.

The Holmburgs were too busy for greetings. Each of them— how many? Seven? Nine? was pulling, pounding, or pushing on the scarred and dented mowing machine, which had come loose from the tractor. Everyone was yelling: "Whoa!" Back up here!" "Come around the other side!" In spite of the volume, I couldn't hear a trace of rancor.

Pleased with my role as observer, I began to sort folks out, starting with an old man in overalls, who had a stoop, a straw hat, no top teeth, and huge hands. Somebody with a high voice called him "Granddaddy." I realized the Holmburgs came in an assortment of sizes—from a short man shaped like a Bosc pear, to a tall slab of a teen-aged boy, to a girl in pink plastic clogs, who might have been five. The concentration of relatives made me feel a surge of homesickness for our own families; a number of our kin, like us, had slipped their moorings and were scattered around the world.

Granddaddy—"Toby" someone else called him—was clearly in charge. Most of the loud directing was coming from him. Second in command was a limber, dark boy, handsome except for teeth that jutted from his mouth like a platform. One man was so thin that his belt made his pants ruffle around his waist. He had a narrow inverted triangle of a face, which ended long before a chin could develop; unlike the graceful boy, he moved in a series of stutters. The little girl had perfect skin and a perfectly round and expressionless face. Her main job seemed to be staying out from under the many-wheeled machinery. Since she wasn't performing any task crucial to the family enterprise, I decided to make her acquaintance.

"Pretty loud, huh?" I said, when she came within earshot. She looked at me without surprise or interest. It wasn't shyness that kept her from answering.

I tried again. "What's your name?"

She put grubby hands on sturdy hips and faced me, blank and silent.

"You can tell her your name." A slightly older girl appeared beside the empty-faced child, taking off heavy leather gloves several sizes too large and wiping her neck with the inside of her wrist. "I'm Rose," she said to me. "You might need to ask her again."

But the little girl spoke. "Penny."

"Penny," I said. "That's pretty."

"No-o," she answered. "PEN-ny."

I looked to Rose for help. She gave me an encouraging smile.

"Peony?" I asked, doubting it.

"Yeah, Penny," the little girl said, and added, "I like horses."

Ah. "Would you like to look at the horses in the barn," I asked.

"Yeah," said Peony, and took my hand.

"Granddaddy doesn't need me right now. Is it all right if I come too?" Rose asked, and we became a threesome.

Standing on the top of a short ladder, holding onto the bars of the stalls which housed Flash, Sandy's sorrel gelding, and my little mare Gwen, Peony confirmed, "I like horses," and then added a variation: "I like these horses." She spoke without inflection, giving each word the same value.

When I asked Rose about school, she painted a happy picture: volleyball, nice teachers—no drugs, she was sure. Her mind was quick, her manners good. She seemed patient with and fond of her—what? Sister? Cousin?

"I want to ride these horses," Peony announced.

"Well, if you come again, maybe we can," I said.

A week later, Peony was back in our yard. The hay was cut and dry, and the Holmburgs had come to bale it. The mower had been replaced with a vintage baler; the noise and most of the people were the same. I recognized Toby, the pear-shaped man, the mis-matched teen-aged boys, Rose and Peony, of course, and the man with no chin. One woman I had not seen. Her short hair was Halloween-black except for an inch next to her scalp, which was white. She seemed friendly, but I had a hard time making out her words, which tumbled in her mouth like hard candy or small stones, like she didn't want me to hear. Then the chinless man came to stand beside her and said something far back in his throat which I couldn't understand at all. When I said, "I'm sorry?" he looked to the black-haired woman, who could have been his sister or mother, as if she might translate for him. Then he

163

tried again, and I was reduced to smiling and nodding assent to what might have been "Let's burn the house down." Recognizing our mutual failure, he went back to the noisy machinery, where everyone strained to communicate.

Discouraged and embarrassed, I went in to the kitchen and brought out the plate of brownies I'd made for dinner. Peony took two, and the black-haired woman asked me for the recipe before rejoining the family effort. I stood and watched the elaborate routine, Toby shouting orders, the others, including Sandy, responding at the same volume, everyone ministering to the venerable, balky baler. Peony, again the only Holmburg unemployed, came and stood beside me, hands, mouth, and dress-front smeared with chocolate. "I like horses," she said.

"Well, maybe," I replied, thinking it would never come to pass, "we can ride one today. We have to wait till there's not so much noise because the horse might be scared."

It was enough of a promise to keep Peony fixed to my side for the rest of the morning. I hadn't wanted a companion, but "Please go away" seemed rude, and I wasn't sure it would have any effect. She came in the house with me, watched while I stacked the books I was considering for fall semester's classes, listened while I made phone calls. At intervals, with unvarying inflection, she repeated her mantra: "I like those horses." Once she asked, "Can I have a drink of that water?"

By the time the tractor and baler rattled across the road to the hay field, accompanied by Sandy and all the Homburgs except Peony, I had run out of tasks and excuses.

"Ok," I said, "you really want to ride a horse?"

Without speaking, she barged out the screen door and marched to the barn. Quiet and expressionless, she watched while I saddled Gwen, the smaller of the two horses. When the dark boy came into the barn in search of a wrench, he said, "'Scuse me, Mam" before asking where to look. I wondered what curious circumstance had make him and Peony part of the same family.

"Ready?" I asked, and she came and stood like a piece of luggage by the horse's side.

"Put me up," she said.

"You have to help, Peony," I told her, and lifted her impassive form till her foot could reach the stirrup. "Swing your leg across," I gasped, pushing on her bottom, and at last she was seated in the saddle, one short, smooth leg sticking out on either side.

"Ready?" I asked again, and Peony nodded. "Hold on here," I pointed to the pommel, and I led the horse around the house.

Most kids new to riding giggle or make cowboy noises. A few want to get off. Peony made no sound. Halfway round the second time, I asked her, "Is this fun?"

"Yeah," she answered. On the strength of that confirmation, I took us on a meandering route behind the barn and through the back pasture, while Peony sat like royalty in the saddle. I doubted that she shared my notion of equality.

When Gwen began to lay back her ears and bite at the lead rope, we returned to the barn and ended the ride. Sandy was in the yard looking tired but pleased. It was quiet. The baler was resting at the edge of the field, and the air was fragrant with hay. Toby's truck was raising dust on the gravel road, and I could just make out the assortment of Homburgs in the back.

"Where are they going?" I asked.

"Home," said Sandy. "They're through for the day." Then, registering Peony, "Oh my gosh. And here's this one."

"Right," I said, putting deep meaning in the word. Peony sat, complacent and silent, on Gwen's back.

"We'll catch them," Sandy said. Gently but quickly, he pulled Peony out of the saddle and hurried to the car.

"Yes, do," I said. I wondered if the Holmburgs were making us a gift of this strange little girl.

I watched the car overtake the truck, both vehicles stop, and the car make a turn and come back.

"What did Toby say?" I asked when they had gone.

Sandy smiled and shook his head. "He said, 'Well, I'll be. We forgot Peony.'"

"Was he upset?"

"Not at all."

"Was Peony?"

"Even less."

I considered how most children of my acquaintance would react if their whole family left them with strangers. Maybe Peony didn't know enough to be scared. Or maybe she knew enough not to be.

During that autumn and winter, we had fairly frequent commerce with the Holmburgs. When we needed to go to a conference or seminar, Sandy would call the Holmburg number and ask for Toby. "Yeah," he'd answer when he came to the phone.

"Toby, this is Sandy."

"Yeah." The inflection was flat, like Peony's; I could hear every word through the phone. I figured he'd answer the queen and the IRS in the same tone.

"Would you all (because no Holmburg ever came alone) be able to take care of our animals next week while we go to Chicago?"

"I reckon," or "Maybe so."

Half an hour later, Toby, the chinless man we now knew as Toby's youngest son, and one or two others would be at our door. "Came to see what needs doing," Toby would say, and Sandy would go over the routine of water, grain, and the vet's phone number.

They were absolutely dependable and did exactly what they were told—nothing less and nothing more. We couldn't bring ourselves to ask them to shovel out the dogs' pens, and they never volunteered, though Toby told us, "We always let 'em out to run. The young'uns like to pet 'em." And the dogs always looked a little plumper when we came back.

Once, and just once, we found that the horse stalls had been meticulously cleaned. When Toby and company dropped by to be sure we'd made it back home, the chinless man let me know he had done the work. The communication took considerable effort on both our parts. His alarmingly narrow jaw smashed his words together and forced them into a kind of gargle. But at last I understood, and thanked him. Then I heard him say, to no one in particular, "That barn needed cleaning," and I felt the reprimand.

Occasionally on weekends when we walked the dogs or rode the horses on the B-level roads, we'd meet a much-used car full of Holmburgs driving slow, on a kind of outing. They always stopped to say "Might rain tonight" or "Corn looks pretty good." Toby usually drove, and beside him usually sat a gray-haired, gray-faced woman he introduced as his wife. Once, he referred to her as "my partner." On our way to Iowa City for a lecture, Sandy pointed out where the Holmburgs lived: three square, white houses, a taller, older farm house, a barn, some outbuildings. I thought of our far-flung family and felt a shiver of envy.

That Fourth of July, I saw the largest gathering of Holmburgs to date. Sandy and I loved the small-town parades and fireworks in the area because they reminded us of Southern celebrations, and we attended two or three each year. In nearby Bellport, population 1,209, he'd gotten the ok to ride his horse in the parade, feeling, he said, much more comfortable in cowboy clothes than in academic regalia. His sister Lucy, visiting from England, was charmed by the concentration of what she called "Americana." She took pictures of the platoon of riding mowers and clapped when the tractors blew bubbles from their exhaust pipes. She spotted the Holmburgs before I did. "Who are those fascinating people?" Lucy asked.

"Oh, it's the Holmburgs," I said, as if that explained everything, and walked over to say hello. Toby was there, and the chinless son, and the dark, slender boy, and several others I knew as part of the family. And there in front of the group was Peony, her hands full of the candy that everyone in the parade was required to throw.

Sure that Peony and I were friends, I squatted beside her and, indicating the collection of Tootsie Pops, M&Ms, and peppermints, said, "Hey Peony, what's your favorite kind?" The candy disappeared behind her, and she looked straight at me with a complete absence of recognition before turning back to the parade. Clearly dismissed, I stood to speak to the others.

Toby raised his finger toward his hat brim but didn't touch it. The chinless man jerked his head in a nod. Then, led by Toby, all the Holmburgs moved slightly away from me. Their group tightened. I was excluded.

Surprised and a little hurt, I crossed the street to rejoin Lucy, who, I realized, had been busily taking pictures of the family. "They just fascinate me," she said. "That little girl—what exactly is wrong with her?" And she leaned forward to get one more shot.

"They're good people," I said. "They help us out." And they're proud, I wanted to add, and they're not an exhibition.

"Well, they're...interesting," said Lucy and waved her fingers at Peony, who, I was glad to see, ignored her.

In late July, the Holmburgs came again to bale the hay. Again, the yard filled with people, shouts, and the clatter of ancient machines. During an enforced pause when the tractor stalled, I chatted with Rose, who was going to play basketball when school started, and a pleasant, stocky woman who identified herself as Rose's mother. She told me that she and her husband—the pear-shaped man, I gathered—had considered moving their children to Arizona—had even taken them out to look for a house. But it didn't feel right out there, and they were back to stay. Rose smiled her relief. When they rejoined the work crew, I felt ashamed of my leisure, and drove to town for an unnecessary trip to the library.

Late that afternoon, I heard Toby's loud knock at the door. It had started to rain, and, he explained, the others had either gone home or to find a part for the mower, which had quit again. He'd stayed to tinker, and some of them would be by in a little bit to pick him up. I remembered when the family had left Peony, but

169

decided Toby was far too important to the Holmburgs' functions to be forgotten. I was more or less getting supper ready, and Sandy was more or less getting ready to go to a meeting, but Toby, unapologetic and completely comfortable, rested the back pockets of his overalls against the kitchen counter, planted his broad hands on the counter's edge, and was there to stay a spell.

"Well," Sandy said, "You've got quite a family, Toby. How many children do you have in all?"

"Nine," Toby answered. "We had nine. And all of us are right there together. Well, except for (he gave two names I didn't catch). They're in Alaska. But they're coming back. Say they miss us."

"So there'll be nine families living on your place. That's almost a town."

"No, now, we're just one family, and some of 'em don't live anywhere. Some of 'em's dead."

"I'm sorry," I said.

"Yeah, one of 'em died the night before he was supposed to get married. Some of us went to look for him and found him sitting on the toilet, dead. He just died there. Supposed to get married the next day."

"That's too bad," Sandy said, and Toby said, "It's a long time ago now." He made a soft noise that sounded like a laugh. "Just died on the toilet." Toby was long on loyalty, short on sentimentality.

The two of them talked about hay for a while—how long it had to dry to keep out mildew, the advantages of big round bales versus small square ones. I chopped onions and sneaked a look at my watch. Toby didn't seem at all concerned about the time. He was where he was.

"Speaking of getting married," Sandy said, "we have to go all the way to England in a couple of weeks, for my sister's wedding.

Toby's "Yeah?" was a request for more information.

Sandy obliged. "Yes, she's been married before."

"Huh," said Toby, and there was a world of opinion in that syllable.

In his sister's defense, Sandy explained, "Her first husband died."

"Yeah," said Toby, apparently satisfied with the explanation. "You can't do nothing about those dead ones."

"How's your wife, Toby?" I asked.

He leaned forward and pulled out a blue handkerchief, wiped his mouth, back and forth, poked the handkerchief back in its pocket.

"They took her off," he said.

"What?"

"Yeah, and she was doing all right too. She'd kind of gotten over that wandering around, gotten used to how she is. They got her in the county home."

"I bet you miss her," I said.

"Do," Toby said. He was quiet for a breath or two before he added, "And it costs a lot more money than having her home."

"That's tough, Toby," Sandy told him. Then, after an appropriate pause, he asked, "Wonder if you all could take care of the animals while we're gone?"

"Don't see why not," Toby answered.

Through the year's seasons, various combinations of Holm-burgs occasionally appeared to water and feed, plant and mow. We received bills printed carefully by hand—Rose's?—and once a phone call explaining patiently that we hadn't signed a check. We noticed that the tall, wide grandson—or nephew—was getting taller and wider. "Yep," said the pear-shaped man, who had to be his father, "we're feeding him toward a basketball scholarship." Once, Peony came along with her grandfather and the son whose face, I decided, was shaped like the blunt side of an axe head. She, like her cousin or brother, had grown, and her smooth, blank quality had intensified. When I spoke to her, she lifted the fingers of one hand without raising her arm. In her other hand, she held a red sucker. I asked if she wanted to look at the horses, and she turned one side to me and concentrated on her candy. Had someone told her not to ask for a ride? Did she associate me with Sandy's sister and her busy camera? Did she remember me at all? In any case, the connection between us had broken, and I felt strangely sad.

One evening at the end of summer, Sandy dialed the now-familiar Holmburg number and asked to speak to Toby. As usual, I could hear both sides of the conversation.

"Toby?"

"Yeah."

"This is Sandy."

"Yeah."

"Wonder if you all could cut our hay again this fall?"

"Well, it'll be a couple of days."

"That's fine."

Toby, who really didn't believe in good-byes, put down the phone. The clatter of the disconnection was loud but not discourteous.

The next morning, I saw a car full of Holmburgs pull into our drive, and soon Toby was pounding on the door with the heel of his hand. He and Sandy walked out in the yard and stood behind the car so they could see the hay field. I came out to be polite and to see what configuration of family Toby was traveling with this time. The pear-shaped man was in the driver's seat and beside him sat the chinless son. In the shadows of the back seat was a person I couldn't identify. Rose and the boys, I figured, were in school. Peony...I wondered about Peony.

Toby, wearing a well-seasoned feed cap, acknowledged me by touching a heavy finger to its bill. "Got my partner with me this time," he said.

"Oh?" I said. "Is that him?" I pointed to the person I didn't know.

"Why, no," Toby said, and smiled as if I'd told a joke, or he had. "That's not a him."

I realized my mistake. "Oh, I'm sorry, it's your wife," I said. "That's great."

"Yep, we went to get her and they said she could come back."

"Is it ok if I speak to her?"

"Sure."

The woman turned a bland face in my direction. Her hair was as weightless and colorless as cobwebs.

"I'm glad to see you again," I said. "I'll bet you're happy to be home."

"Yes," she said. "It was good to go and visit for a while, and then when I saw what there was to see, I was ready to leave."

Was this the dementia talking, or had she always been this way? In her I saw an older, more cheerful version of Peony.

Hay business settled, Toby got in the back seat beside his wife.

"Yep, got my partner back," he said before he closed the door. He covered his wife's hand with his, then took it quickly away.

Touched, I said, and meant it, "I'm so glad to see you all together again."

"Yeah," said Toby, "it's good for a family to be together." He slammed his door, then rolled down the window.

"Cheaper too," he said, and the Holmburgs drove away.

Lucy's Scarf

It was about 9:30PM (pretty late for me). My husband and I, teachers who have taken up small-scale farming, were waiting to meet his sister Lucy at the airport in Des Moines. Lucy was a New York expatriate living just outside of Cambridge, England, where her late husband had been a venerated teacher of literature at that university. Lucy accompanies bel canto singers on the piano, volunteers at the elegant Fitzwilliam Museum, and holds soirées in her back garden. She visits us twice a year, and I dread each visit.

Still, Lucy and I are friends. When she comes to Iowa, I look forward to long walks and talks with this perfectly nice woman. But every time Sandy and I pick her up in the Des Moines International Airport, she commits the same sin: She makes me feel dowdy. This time, however, I thought I was well prepared. Before leaving our farmhouse in the dead center of Iowa, I'd put on my newest Polartec pants and my beaver earmuffs. I had changed the boots I use for barn work. I had fluffed up my down jacket and refreshed my ChapStick. As an accessory, I had brought a thick biography of Victor Hugo instead of the mystery I was really reading.

Then Lucy appeared, smiling, in a soft black sweater and trousers—not pants—and a taupe—not tan—coat. Her hair curled softly and obediently; eight hours on the plane had not flattened a tendril. Her black pumps had just the right amount of shine, just the right amount of heel. I hugged her; she was delicately fragrant.

Her presence transformed me. Moments before, I'd felt pretty good. I'd been surrounded by pleasant, practical people dressed intelligently in lined jeans and long, thick scarves, and I had blended comfortably into the environment. Lucy's appearance changed us all—me especially—into country mice. I resented the transformation.

Since everything I wanted to say began with "Damn it, Lucy," instead I said, "What a beautiful scarf." It was an inane statement but a true one, and better than the alternatives. Indeed, Lucy—like so many of us—was wearing a piece of fabric around her throat, but it was draped, not wrapped, and it was a William Morris print silk, not navy wool or polyester fleece. The blues, greens, and creams of it rippled as she walked. Ridiculously, I decided that scarf made the difference between Lucy's appearance and mine, between Lucy's *life* and mine, and I told her again how much I admired it.

"I like it too," she said. "It was a gift from my friend Patricia—you remember, the publisher who has the little place in Ireland. She's so generous, sometimes it's embarrassing." I did remember meeting Lucy's rather famous and flamboyant friend; the memory did not improve my mood.

We loaded Lucy's slender bags in the car, and I insisted on riding in the back seat. I wanted to deal with my petty thoughts, and to give brother and sister a chance to talk. Typically, Lucy asked about our news: Did we still enjoy the small, intense college where we'd taught for decades? Was our little string band still performing in the coffee shop? And then they settled in to discuss Dad. Though Sandy and I are certainly one reason for Lucy's trips to Iowa, she comes most of all to see their 97-year old father, who lives gracefully in a retirement home near us. An hour on Interstate 80 through Iowa's dark winter fields brought us to the Mayflower's guest room that Lucy always occupies. We walked together to Dad's apartment, where we left the two to a happy reunion.

I spent part of the next morning wrestling with envy and covetousness, sins much more deadly than any Lucy had committed, and by the time I called her at noon, I'd had what seemed like a little victory: Lucy's visits, I reasoned, were just infrequent enough to let me forget how different, how foreign she seemed to me. Not foreign to her upbringing in the South, which she and her brother—now my husband—and I myself had experienced. Not foreign in the sense of English; I knew people in England who could pass, though unwillingly, for Midwesterners. This was not true of Lucy. Each time she arrived, she seemed to have come from a land where perfection was possible, where no one watched sports on TV or read bad novels or ate candy bars, to name a few of my minor transgressions. This impression always lessened in the days she spent with us, but it did not disappear.

My insulated mittens seemed bulky, so I put on my leather gloves for the quick drive from our farm to Dad's place. Tapping on the door, I walked in to find father and daughter lingering over a late breakfast. Dad was handsome as always, in a soft blue shirt and a tie. Lucy was as close as she can get to dishabille. In her dressing gown—not a bathrobe—and without makeup, she looked a little tired. But still...arranged, collected, composed. I decided she was incapable of sloppiness, that she simply could not wear the knits and Nikes I relied on. Nevertheless, we had a pleasant visit. Dad lovingly pointed out the parallels between Lucy's life and mine: college connections, music, and even volunteer work, since I'd recently joined the board of our local museum. I was certain my gentle father-in-law was unaware of the irony in the comparisons, starting with grand Cambridge University and tiny Grinnell College.

Lucy, as always, had come bearing gifts. Mine was a package of beautiful note cards from the Fitzwilliam. Months ago, I'd mentioned how much I admired hers, and she never forgets such a hint. Then, she and Dad proudly revealed their project for the three weeks of Lucy's stay: they were going to read aloud all of James' *Portrait of a Lady*. When Dad left the room, Lucy told me that Dad was already concerned about poor Isabel Archer, beguiled by a way of life that didn't exist. Always tender toward her father, she hoped he wouldn't worry too much about Isabel's illusions. I left for a tennis game, hoping my long-time opponent would feel tender toward me.

The few weeks of Lucy's visit passed quickly. The four of us had congenial gatherings—take-out Chinese at Dad's apartment, a leisurely afternoon at our farm house, where we sang old hymns and took Dad to see our small herd of longhorns. Lucy and I mapped out a two-mile route through what she called the pretty part of town, and we walked together as often as she could bear to leave her father. On our first outing, she asked about our three grandchildren, and said someday she hoped to have some of her own. Her son, who still lives in Manhattan, has had liaisons with several gorgeous women, none of them permanent. I told her we were going to keep the grandkids while Ruben and Gina spent a night out to celebrate their anniversary. She told me she was taking her son to Paris on the Eurostar for his birthday. I wondered again about irony.

On another walk, when I asked her about the latest soirée, she laughed and said, "Isn't that funny? We use that word as a joke. We just do some readings—some Shakespeare or a poem someone's working on—and I play and Eleanor sings Verdi or Puccini." And later she volunteered that Patricia's place in Ireland was "just a small house really, nothing like an estate."

Somehow this genteel modesty and self-effacement only made Lucy's world seem more attractive. At home that night, I had to remind myself of some important truths: I have an excellent husband, some very good friends, two good dogs, a few good acres of land, and a pretty good horse. My grandchildren live nearby. I would trade my full and steady life with no one. Besides, I'd be uncomfortable in Lucy's world of music and travel and poetry. I'd be conspicuous, awkward, a hayseed.

But maybe if I had the right clothes....

One day, I suggested varying our usual route: We could come to our place and take Hyde and Sheik, our two big Labs, through the paths Sandy has made in the prairie we're restoring. Lucy was game, and did her best to dress for a slog through the concoction of mud and snow that is Iowa's winter specialty. But her best was way too good—thin leather boots and that fine taupe coat she'd arrived in. I insisted on outfitting her, and soon she was bundled up in insulation and Gor-tex—and, somehow, she managed to bring a measure of elegance to the bulky garb.

When we finished our trek, she said something that startled me: "I envy you for knowing where your home is. I'm not sure how long I'll stay in Cambridge. Maybe I'll move back to New York. Maybe," she said, smiling, "Maybe I'll come here to retire."

In the last week of Lucy's stay, the two of us were invited to lunch by my friend Wendy. A lawyer by profession and a musician by avocation, Wendy had attended a singing class in Cambridge the previous summer. At my suggestion, she had called Lucy and they'd gone together to Evensong at King's Chapel. We three arranged to meet at our little town's one good restaurant, and I looked forward to the event.

I finished cleaning horse stalls and dog pens in plenty of time to shower and dress. Though it was cold and I was tempted to don my usual layers, I decided to aim for a sleeker look. I could hear my mother saying, "One good piece can make an outfit," so I pinned her gold reciter's medal to my dark red sweater. Looking in the mirror, I could hear her voice: "You look very nice."

Lucy arrived at the restaurant a few minutes after Wendy and me. We exchanged cordial greetings, decided it was an occasion and ordered wine, and began the easy, pleasant talk of women who like each other. It was chilly in the restaurant, and Lucy kept on her coat. Wendy and Lucy talked about a chamber ensemble they both admired and the acoustics in King's Chapel. When they asked me about our band's next performance, I was amused, not irritated, by the contrast. We all laughed at the possibility of including Hank Williams and Vaughan Williams in the same program.

Just before our salads came, Lucy slipped off her coat. She was wearing the William Morris scarf. I looked nice. She looked lovely.

We lingered over salmon; we had another glass of wine. I felt like a character in a one-act play, a supporting character. Finally, Wendy said, "I hate to break up this party, but I have to get back to the real world of work." Lucy excused herself—to pick up the check, I knew—and Wendy asked, "What does she think of us here? We must seem like a bunch of clods to her."

"Oh no," I said, and had no idea if it was true.

The museum board was meeting on the morning Lucy had to catch her plane back to England, so she and Sandy made the trip to Des Moines alone. I was glad not to witness the brave, sad parting between Lucy and her father. And I was sorry that her visit was over. Sandy had described her as an "easy keeper," and we'd smiled at the implied comparison between Lucy and livestock.

At supper that night, Sandy reported that Lucy had only cried a little when she left, and that she planned to come back in the Spring. "And she left you this," he said, handing me a small plastic bag with "Caviar House" printed elegantly upon it.

I opened it, and the scarf poured out onto the table.

"I am really embarrassed," I said. "I practically begged your sister for this scarf." And, terrified that a fold would dip in the chili, I put it quickly back into its bag.

The next day I got the scarf out, intending to wear it. Then I reviewed my agenda: put up flyers downtown for the weaving demonstration at the museum, attend the class I was auditing at the college, where the dress code is jeans and flannel; and play another fierce game of tennis. The scarf didn't fit my schedule. It didn't fit me—as Lucy's life didn't fit me—or my life her. I considered sending it back to her, but decided I would keep Lucy's generous gift as a talisman against envy. And because it was beautiful.

Mirror, Mirror

Bereft, I decided. Betrayed and bereft best described how I felt. We'd had a perfectly good relationship for twenty years, and now he was leaving. He said he needed a change, a new beginning. For me, the idea of starting over was painful. How would I even begin to find someone else to cut my hair?

I had gone to Merle's small, sunny shop every month for the two decades I'd lived and taught in Grinnell, a tiny town that housed a college of the same name. Merle's great skill lay not in cutting hair but in tailoring his conversations to fit each of his customers. He could be gossipy, sympathetic, bawdy, or restrained depending on who was sitting in his barber's chair, facing his flattering, pink-tinted mirror. With me, he was restrained. He'd adopted that attitude from the moment I confessed that I taught composition and Intro to Literature at the college.

Since then, he'd told me a series of bland jokes and stories that he judged appropriate for a lady of my profession. I had nodded and smiled, and, though we weren't friends, exactly, we had gotten along very well. Now he was leaving to start a new life, and I was in mourning. The fact that the only other hair-cutting establishment in town was the Hair Doctor, staffed by a bevy of young female self-styled stylists, added to my grief.

It wasn't that I missed Merle's predictable, sometimes haphazard haircuts; what I dreaded was constructing a new social situation. How would I talk to my next—What: Barber? Beautician? I didn't even know the right title. Nothing, I had discovered long ago, stymies conversation so quickly as the words, "I teach English." People immediately become self-conscious, sullen, and bored. Years of dealing with such reactions, plus a natural reticence, have made me a rather quiet person. Some people, I'm well aware, consider me a prude, or worse, a snob.

In fact, I long to be able to participate in the easy, back-and-forth conversations I overhear among my students and between acquaintances in grocery and video stores: "So, what's been going on with you?" or "Girl (or Man), you would not believe. It's been wild, you know what I'm saying?" I envy this improvised banter, but simply cannot copy it. Some people can't dance; I can't chat. I can't catch the rhythm that reminds me of scat singing, another art beyond my reach. Perhaps the study of grammar has made me formal and stiff. My disability is especially apparent in beauty salons, where I'm surrounded by people who seem to have perfected this kind of talk, and can punctuate it with meaningful looks and laughter.

And I confess to an uglier concern: How could I endure the loud and error-ridden babble I would undoubtedly hear month after month from a collection of cosmetologists? I would be besieged by phrases like "going to the movie with he and I," discussions of grandpa's "prostrate" cancer, and the high drama of whether glitter nail polish was appropriate for a wedding. Apparently, in the core of my English-teaching heart, I am a snob.

Unfazed by my dilemma, my hair soon reached a state of emergency. A colleague, whose hair, like mine, is kinky or lank, depending on the humidity, said she'd had good luck with Patty at the Hair Doctor. With trepidation, I called for an appointment.

My palms were damp when I entered the building whose signs offered tropical tans and artificial nails. The receptionist encouraged me to have a cappuccino from the gurgling machine and wait "just a tiny bit." In a few minutes, Patty made her entrance. It was "Pati," actually, I learned from her nametag, and I wondered if she'd been born with an "i" and one "t." I knew her carefully casual blonde hair wasn't a birthright. "Blowsy" was the adjective I attached to Pati.

She ushered me to her chair and, in a voice trained to be heard over dryers and running water, asked me about my hopes for my hair. Then she led me to the shampoo sink. My hair cleansed, she repositioned me in front of the big blue-white mirror, separated my hair into symmetrical patches and began to cut—in silence. All around us pairs of stylists and clients were chatting and laughing. I could hear fragments: "and then she told him…," "I just said *Whatever*…." Ours was the only quiet cubicle. Pati was chewing gum and leaving the conversation to me. I decided it was either a power play or that the head under those blonde curls was empty. As I often did in an unresponsive classroom, I succumbed to the pressure and caved in.

"Is that your dog?" I asked, referring to a picture of a perky beagle taped to the edge of the mirror. I thought, "Please let her answer be longer than "yes." My fingers were tight on the arms of the swivel chair.

"You bet, that's Tulip. I just got her last week and she's...." Pati was off, and I listened, immensely relieved, to vignettes of Tulip's chewing socks, whining, and digging holes under the fence. It wasn't Shakespeare but at least we weren't sitting in tomb-like quiet, and I didn't have to reveal my lack of skill in the conversational equivalent of volleyball—or my lack of interest in the narrative. And the fact that we saw each other refracted through the mirror created a comfortable distance between us.

When we'd temporarily exhausted the topic of Tulip, I asked about the little boy with the wide, snaggled smile whose photo was just under the beagle.

"That's Trent," Pati said. "Cute, huh? He mostly stays with Mom and Dad. My cousin had him when she was fifteen, so the whole family shares him. He sometimes don't know who he belongs to, but in Trent's case, that's not all bad." Then she added that she, Trent, and her dad were going up to Minnesota to see the Vikings play. I said, "It's good of you to go with the fellows."

"Oh no," she said. "I'm the fan. The guys just tag along."

Well, I thought, this is distinctly better than discussing the color of nail polish. And just maybe this person is not so predictable as her hair and name suggest. Maybe there's a story here, and maybe I'll get to hear it. She held a hand mirror to show me the back of my new haircut. It looked good.

When I glanced at the note Pati had written at the bottom of my receipt, I was happy to see that "thanks" didn't end in an x, and the circle she used as a dot above her name contained no smiley face. I'd survived my first session at the Hair Doctor. I made another appointment.

Four weeks later, when I sat again in front of Pati's mirror watching her trap tufts of my hair between her middle and index fingers, I went straight for our established subject. "So how's Tulip?" I asked. I'd picked up the initial "So" (no pause) from her.

"Oh, let me tell you, that dog. She ate a washcloth. And mad, I was so mad—not at Tulip. Al just left it out on the porch of that old Victorian house of mine, and of course Tulip ate it. I was just in time to see the corner with the label disappear into her little pink mouth. And I told him if that dog got sick, he could just reconsider his residency at my house."

I was rafting down Pati's stream of consciousness, trying to get an oar in the water. "Who's Al?" I asked

"Oh, my old boyfriend. He showed up again. I don't know if it's good or bad, but I guess we're kind of engaged. It's OK, I guess. Charlie and Tulip get along real well."

"Ah...who's Charlie?" I was aware that Pati had the verses and I had the chorus.

"Oh, his puppy. He's cute, so I guess they can stay."

Pati's pronouns added mystery to her narrative, in the manner of Henry James, but I figured "he" was Charlie, and "they" were dog and boyfriend, and that the occupancy of Pati's house had doubled.

"Got big plans for the weekend?" she asked as she released me from my cape. It was a formula, I knew, and she didn't want much information. But I thought I owed her something in exchange for the characters and setting she'd given me. "I'm going to hear a string quartet at the college," I told her.

"Oh, nice," she said, making the words sound like condolence. "Have a good one."

This haircut cost me three dollars more than the first one, but my hair looked ok, and Pati's story was better than the papers I'd been grading on *The Great Gatsby*. I told her I'd see her in about a month.

I went alone to the concert but walked part way home with a young visiting professor. He dispelled every bit of Vivaldi's magic by complaining about the students in his seminar, who "don't know Steinbeck from Stendhal or where to find the front door of the library." I thought wistfully of Pati's upbeat patter.

When I returned to the Hair Doctor, Pati greeted me with "And how was that music you went to see?" I was flattered that she remembered. After I told her that the music was fine and I'd just have the usual, please, she volunteered that "Tulip's good, but Charlie's having some kind of adjustment problem." My concerns about conversation had all but vanished, though I was aware I wasn't contributing much. I was also aware that compared to the adventures of Pati and company, my predictable academic life was a poor pale thing.

"What's up with Charlie?" I said, echoing the phrasing I was hearing around me.

"He's marking everything," Pati answered, her voice loud with indignation. "The rugs, the plants, the steer-eo. I've worked my tail off on that old house, and I told Al he'd have to change that dog's behavior. I told him flat out that if this keeps up, I'll have him cut."

For one amazing moment, I thought Pati was going to have Al neutered. But then the pronouns fell into place.

"You really have a full house," I offered, hoping for more.

"Tell me about it. From one to five or six in two months."

"Five or six? Have you gotten more dogs?"

"Oh no," Pati shook her blonde do. "Al's two youngest kids have moved in. But the seventeen-year-old still spends a lot of time with her mom, who lives just down the block. Which is good, since she's too old to train."

The daughter, I figured, not the mom. "Uh, how many kids does Al have?" I asked. I'd given up trying to sound cool. I just wanted to hear this story unfold and learn more about the characters.

"Just three," Pati said. "The oldest's a boy, but he's not around much. He left when Al started drinking again."

Again, I thought, but didn't say.

"He's stopped for good now, I guaran-absolutely-tee you."

Maybe Pati hadn't been threatening to cut the dog.

"He's been a real good daddy to Sybil. She's a good kid too, for a ten-year-old."

"So, you have a new—can I say 'daughter'?"

Pati stopped cutting. Our eyes connected in the mirror, and I could see her considering the relationship. I thought, too, that I'd glimpsed a kind of intimacy between us.

"Well, yeah, I guess so." Her scissors started again. "She gets along fine with Tulip and Charlie, and she'll keep her clothes picked up now because Tulip ate a pair of her socks and then threw up in the middle of her bed."

Sybil's bed, I imagined.

My hair was still pretty short when I called for my next appointment, but I couldn't wait any longer for another installment, or to experience again the easy connection I'd begun to feel with Pati. One lonely afternoon, I'd even thought briefly of asking if she'd like to meet for coffee, an invitation I'd certainly never issued to Merle. But I decided she might feel awkward in the absence of combs, capes, and mirrors.

A voice said, "Hello, Hair Doctor, nails, and tanning this is Lindsey how can I help you?" No inflection, no punctuation. Three days later, I was back in Pati's chair.

"That must be Sybil," I half stated, half asked. Another picture had joined the gallery on Pati's mirror. I was draped again in a dark, crinkly cape that opened at the back, a kind of reverse Three Musketeers effect. My already short hair was being made shorter still. "You got it," Pati said. "She's right up there with Tulip." I wondered if she meant on the mirror or in her affections. Listening to Pati was rather like being in a play, I thought, complete with characters and dialogue. As usual, Pati had the lead.

"I have to tell you that that brave dog chased up a huge old blue herring that was wading in the creek behind Dad's house. Why, that bird could have lifted that dog right off the ground."

I was charmed rather than irritated by Pati's diction, and wondered what use Dorothy Sayers might make of a red heron.

"But you need to know, last week, Sibyl's picture was in danger of coming down."

"Really?" I asked.

"Really!" Patti answered me. I thought we sounded like confidants. "She spent the weekend with her mom, and came home with new underwear and a serious question for her dad and I. That's what she said, 'I have a serious question for you guys.' I told her to wait till dinner, so at the table she put her hands flat down on either side of her plate and said, 'My mom wants to know when you're going to let me start dating.' Al said, 'Dating? You're ten. Don't even think about it,' and she slapped her hands down on the table and flounced out of the room. He and I just stared at each other for a minute and then he shoved back his chair and started after her, breathing fire. Tulip and Charlie hid under the table."

"Dogs know when there's trouble," I said.

"Yeah. Well, I said, 'Wait now, you both need to cool off,' and he turned around and slammed out the door. In a little bit, here she came, wanting to show me what her mom had bought her. She spread those things out on the table, and would you believe?"

Here, Pati lowered her voice to tell the shocking secret. I glanced at the mirror and saw two women, two friends, perhaps, connected in a private exchange. It could have been a scene from a novella.

"Those things were thongs, and string thongs at that. In a ten-year-old size. And just then Tulip and Charlie zipped out from under the table and Charlie stopped just long enough to mark the chair I was sitting in. Mad? I cannot tell you."

Giddy with the narrative's speed, I made a bold move. "Well," I said, "You might use the thongs on Charlie, kind of like diapers."

Pati held her scissors up and tilted her head. If Tulip had told a joke, I think she would have been less surprised. In the mirror, I saw her shake her head. Then she laughed a short, loud laugh, and I laughed with her.

"I might of considered it," she said, "but when Al came back in, he took a fork and picked those things up one at a time and dropped them in the garbage. I think we've seen the last of those little items."

At the counter when I gave Pati my credit card, she said, "I guess the wedding will be in a couple of months." For the time it took to slide my card, I thought she might invite me, but as she handed me the slip to sign, the intimacy I had imagined in the mirror was gone. Still, she had told me her secret.

"Have a nice day, now," she said.

As I was going out the door, I heard Pati's next client exclaim, "Well, girl, I can't wait to hear what Al said when Sybil fished those sweet little thongs out of the trash."

Brothers

Wade and Charles Ferguson were brothers, born of a stern father and a soft, sweet mother on a red clay farm in western North Carolina. Charles was six years younger than Wade, and in between them there was a short, soft brother, Randolph, who didn't seem to matter much. Scattered among the boys were three sisters, who Wade and Charles liked all right when they thought about them.

In spite of their age difference, Charles and Wade grew up to look like mirror images—Black Irish, folks said, with their blue eyes and dark wavy hair. "Strapping boys," they said. "Make Mr. Hamp a couple of good hands." The big difference between them was that, from the beginning, Wade worked hard to please others—his parents, his teachers, the neighbors who came to visit on Sunday afternoons—and Charles never meant to please anybody but himself.

When Wade was seven and Charles had just begun to walk, Wade nailed one of his mother's empty wooden spools on the screen door at just the right height for his brother's sticky baby hand. To the end of his life, Wade remembered what his father had said to his wife: "Miss Lula, that boy's right smart." It was the only kind thing he ever heard his father say about him.

In Mr. Hamp's defense, it was not a time when fathers were kind to their sons. Farmers, especially, expected their boys to be hard-working, respectful, obedient hands. When their father called them at 4:30 AM on pale summer mornings, Charles and Wade knew to get up quick, before they heard Mr. Hamp's feet on the stairs. He'd be coming, they knew, with a razor strop in his hand. Randolph got up too, of course, but what good was he? Too short to harness the mule, not strong enough to hold the plow handles steady. The girls, Rosser, Hayes, and Nina, could sleep until just light, but then, they were girls.

When did the love between the two brothers start? When Wade nailed Charles's spool to the door? When did the rivalry begin? Did they vie to see who could lift the heaviest stones from the rocky red fields they plowed? Did they compete for their sweet mother's love?

One of Wade's most vivid memories of Miss Lula was that, unlike Mr. Hamp, she never got mad at her children. But sometimes, if one of them had left a task undone or if she overheard them squabbling, she'd get sad, and, for Wade at least, that was far worse than anger. When she got sad, Miss Lula would go to the barn, climb to the hay loft, and pull the ladder up after her. The children, all six of them, would gather where the feet of the ladder had rested and look up at the loft window, listening to their mother cry. They'd promise to be good and beg her to come down, but she'd stay up there until her sadness had passed.

Wade often told of standing with the others, calling up to Mama, until the ladder reappeared and their mother was among them again. Only Charles refused to promise Miss Lula never to be bad again. He waited with the others but he waited in silence, too proud, Wade knew, ever to beg.

Charles liked to tell the story of their mother peeling apples: "She would take the knife and go round and round each apple, so she made one long curly strip that never broke. And that strip was all thin and red because she never cut into the apple's meat. Just pure peel would unwind, and I'd hold up my hands to catch it. Nobody else was there, just me and her."

The brothers shared—and sometimes spoke about—one more vivid recollection of their mother, one that was painful to Charles. Two tomcats had been howling for several nights outside Miss Lula and Mr. Hamp's bedroom window, and one morning, the children heard her say, "I wish somebody'd get rid of those cats." Charles, on this particular occasion, intending to please his mother, caught the cats, tied their tails together, and threw them over the clothesline, one on either side. Right away, he knew he'd made a mistake. Screaming and hissing, the cats tore each other to shreds. Miss Lula was horrified. Charles, when he'd tell the story, shook his head.

Maybe because of their mother, all their lives, Wade and Charles liked women—in the man-woman sense, certainly, but also they just liked them: their smallness, their gentleness, their fresh smell and sweet voices. From the first, Wade was monogamous. He favored blue-eyed Betsy from the neighboring farm, and then Cora from Sunday School, and then.... He married and lived with his wife Jane for fifty-two years.

Charles liked womankind. He spoke of sitting in the school gymnasium in the winter, watching the girls play basketball.

The only heat came from a fat wood-burning stove at one end of the court, and the girls would cluster around its warmth during breaks in the game. "Their legs would get red and dry," Charles said, "and they'd get those little diamond-shaped cracks in their skin." He filled his eyes with women. Charles was married once, for about seven months, to a woman named Linda. He never spoke of her and her name rarely came up in family stories. Having tried marriage, for the rest of his life he courted an array of women—Virginia, with the sultry voice and the thick curly hair; Norma Womble, who brought him coconut cakes; slim, sweet-voiced Marie, who sometimes came to Sunday dinner. Often, when a sister would answer the phone and Miss Lula would ask, "Who is it?" the reply was "One of Charles's women."

Was Wade envious? In later years, would he have traded his safe married state for Charles's reckless, varied Saturday nights? At least once in a while? It was a question I sometimes pondered because I was Wade's daughter, and I wouldn't have existed if Wade had been more like Charles in affect as well as in looks.

In my mind, my father and my uncle were the world's most handsome men. From their father, they had each inherited height, stern blue eyes, common sense, and a love of horses. They both liked to tell stories of Dan, the black Percheron, who could out-pull any horse in the county, of Bess and Boy, who took the children—often riding double—to school, waited patiently at the hitching rail, and brought them home again.

When I was five, the brothers bought a pair of gaited saddle horses, shiny, spirited sorrels, whom they named Lady Margaret and Lady Flash, otherwise known as the Ladies. What a picture those two black-haired men made on those red horses. Awe and pleasure almost kept me from breathing when they came down the driveway in a clattering rack. Were they racing? Was it a contest? How could it not be? I only knew my pure and desperate joy when my mother handed me up to my father and he put me in front of him on the saddle. No one else in the family ever got to ride those horses—not my mother, who might have liked to, not the sisters, who would have refused, not short, soft Randolph, who sat on the front porch and talked. Only my father, my uncle, and I.

Miss Lula often praised her children, telling them they were "good and sweet." If Mr. Hamp praised at all, it was indirect. "Well, you didn't shame me, boy" he would tell Wade when he brought home good grades from school or fixed the pump handle on the cistern. Still, Wade worked hard to satisfy his father, and in that way, usually avoided his stern parent's wrath.

Not so Charles. Mr. Hamp often whipped this proud, stubborn son—with a belt, a razor strop, and rope. When Charles was fifteen and he had failed to do his chores, Mr. Hamp, holding a bridle rein he was oiling, told him to take off his shirt for a beating.

"No Sir," Charles said and grabbed his father's wrist. The two strong men leaned into each other until the older man's arm began to tremble. When Mr. Hamp dropped the rein, Charles stooped and gave it back to him. "You won't ever whip me again," he said, and slowly walked back to the barn to milk the cows.

I heard that story twice—two slightly different versions on two far-apart summer evenings. Each time, a small gathering of family members were sitting outside on folding lawn chairs, as was the custom. Charles and my father had just mowed the lawn.

They were nearly identical in their khaki overalls, except that Daddy wore a golf cap because he'd begun to lose his thick black hair. And the two brothers rode two different makes of mowers, and favored two different styles of mowing. But they were each holding a beer they reckoned they'd earned. Both times Charles told the story with a mixture of pride and sadness. Charles and Daddy had loved Mr. Hamp in the way they were taught to love God—with a love that was very close to fear; they had to wait till their father was dead to bring beer home. They remembered him as a stern but not a cruel man. Each had responded to the sternness as his nature allowed.

My uncle and my father also enjoyed drinking hard liquor. Daddy, whose career was teaching agriculture to high school boys in a nearby town, drank in a literally measured way: two jiggers of Kentucky Gentleman mixed with 7-Up on Friday and Saturday nights, two beers on Sunday afternoons. He knew very well that alcohol and school teaching were mutually exclusive, and he guarded his reputation carefully. Drink made Daddy talkative. When the people around him grew tired of listening, he'd pick up the phone, call an old buddy, and talk for an hour. "Wade," Charles would ask him, "Don't your mouth get tired?"

Over his Sunday beers, Charles, a silent rather than a quiet man, loosened up just enough to tell a story now and then— always a powerful one. On the occasions when Charles talked, we all listened. I never saw Charles drink anything except those beers, but I knew, from hints and references, that for years his drinking had been extreme and, occasionally, dangerous. When the talk turned to horses on those Sunday evenings, one sister or the other might say, "Remember when Charles and his crowd

used to ride all night and then go right to work in the morning?"
I inferred, correctly, that Charles's work—he had held a variety
of jobs: dairy farming, foreman at the chicken plant, loading
trucks at the grain store—frequently took second place to his
drinking. Then one summer he suddenly quit—something about
Daddy bailing him out of trouble, if not jail—and his consump-
tion of alcohol became even more measured than his brother's.
But always, drinking or not, there was in Charles's attitude that
hinted-at recklessness and freedom.

One day, when I was six and my cousin Gwynne was ten,
Charles somehow had been given charge of us for the afternoon.
I suspect my mother and father were doing something respectable—helping out at the high school—and the aunts may have
thought that making Charles a babysitter was funny. My uncle
chose his cars like he did his horses—they had to be big, fast, and
showy. So Gwynne and I were delighted to find ourselves in the
backseat of Charles's long gold Chrysler. No one had thought of
seatbelts yet and we slid from one door to the other as Charles
negotiated the curves on the way in to town.

At the drugstore, he ordered three Coca-Colas in green glass
bottles and then gave Gwynne and me each a quarter so we
could shop in the toy aisle. We must have spent an hour looking
at tops and water pistols and comic books. Used to being hurried
along by an impatient parent, we found this freedom deliciously
extravagant. Charles seemed perfectly content to give us our
leisure—he had to do something with his two unaccustomed
charges—and the black-haired woman behind the counter
seemed glad for his company. In the end, Gwynne and I each
chose a tin whirligig—the 1950s version of those colorful plastic

pinwheels on a stick that children now blow on or run with to make them spin. We had tested every one of them in the store to make sure we got the ones that spun the fastest.

Did Charles talk to us on the way home? I don't remember that he said a word. But when he turned onto the gravel road to Gwynne's house, where other adults would relieve him of his duty, he said, "Hold on." Rocks hit the underside of the Chrysler like bullets; pine trees blurred into a film of green and brown. I grabbed for Gwynne's hand, but he was rolling down his window, and understanding his plan, I did the same. The wind smacked our faces. We nodded to each other and at the same moment stuck our pinwheels out into the gale. They didn't last a second. We didn't even see our bright toys sail away. All we held were the ends of the snapped wands. And all we felt was joy. What better proof of the speed Charles had created? What better souvenirs than our splintered wooden sticks?

Of course, when Charles pulled up in the driveway and turned to look at us, we understood that we could show our sticks to no one. What had happened that day was a secret between Charles and the two of us. And our adventure was complete.

The only other escapade Charles took me on happened 15 years later. I had brought the man I meant to marry home to meet and be approved of by the family, and Charles said to the two of us (Was it a test?) "You want to go riding this evening?"

"Sure," we said in unison, and around 6:00 PM, we got into the most recent version of the Chrysler to drive to Lacey Womble's pasture. Daddy came along, not to ride—he was "down in the back"—but to see what Lacey had these days in the way of horses. He'd put one of the folding lawn chairs in the boot of the car.

I remember that Daddy was wearing his golf cap. Charles usually scorned head gear, though he always wore a knit cap to bed to keep his waves under control. It was fragrant with hair oil. Recently, I'd heard Daddy say, "Well, he's kept his hair, but he's losing his hearing." Was it a game? Did they both keep score?

Three men were waiting when we got to the red metal gate. They greeted my uncle and father, then nodded to Sandy and me. Lacey carried a bucket of sweet feed.

"Might have to coax 'em some," he said. "Haven't had a saddle on 'em in a couple of months."

Daddy opened his chair, and I stayed with him while the others walked out in the pasture, Lacey whistling the two-note call everybody used to call horses in. And they came thundering, red mud caked on their legs, cockleburs matted in their manes. They were skittish and snorty, but soon six of them had halters on.

"Give Prince to Miss Betty," Lacey said. "He's dead broke."

Prince did not look "bullet proof" to me (our other label for a gentle horse). He jerked back on the reins when Charles threw the saddle on his back, and bunched up when he felt the girth pulled tight.

"Want a leg up?" Charles asked, and I found myself sitting on that big restless gelding, who did not seem pleased to have me there.

"Wish I could ride him for you, little girl," my father said. "Wish I was going along."

I wasn't sure if he was worried about me or sad that he was being left out.

Then we were ready—me on Prince and Sandy on a gray horse with a blaze face. Sandy looked both grim and excited. I was determined to keep Prince in the rear, at least until I got a feel for him, but that was not an option. He knew his place—one back from the lead horse, which Charles, of course was riding—and he muscled his way into that position. When Charles's black mare began to canter, Prince matched her speed and the others followed. The horses tossed their heads; the men shouted.

"If I die," I thought, "I'll be in good company," and then, because I had no chance of controlling any part of the situation, I relaxed into Prince's power. A slight mist magnified the lightening bugs into soft miniature headlights and intensified the sweet smells of honeysuckle and horse sweat. We clattered down rocky banks and splashed through creeks. We ducked under oak branches and got switched hard in the face by pine boughs. When the horses began to lather, we finally slowed to a walk. I had nothing to do with where we went or how fast we got there. Before it got completely dark, Charles had glanced back at me twice, and I'd nodded back at him. Sandy rode beside me, his eyes big, his smile wide. I loved him for loving our wild ride.

Daddy was in the car when we got back. "Rode hard, I see," he said, looking at the drying sweat on the horses' necks and flanks. "You and Sandy stayed on, did you?" he asked me, and I could see how much it hurt him not to be riding with us. When he offered to take Prince's saddle off, Charles said, "You just sit down, Brother, rest your back," and he slung the heavy saddle into the bed of Lacey's truck as if it were a bag of rice.

It had been a glory of a ride. I gave Prince a farewell pat on the neck and whispered a "thank you" for tolerating his clumsy burden. I was proud of Sandy, proud of myself, and grateful to Charles for letting us be part of his rowdy group.

Then I looked at Daddy in the car and understood how he felt his exclusion, was shamed by his ailing body, his lessening strength. He must have been hot in the car. Mosquitoes must have found him. He could have driven home—Charles had left his keys in the ignition—but I'd have been surprised. He was like that—dependable, responsible, steady. He was my father. But Charles was my hero.

When Charles died, it was quick and hard—an aneurism, a stroke, a fitful, angry day in the hospital—and that was it. Sandy and I were in England teaching for a semester, so I heard the news from my cousins. Apparently, Charles and Daddy had had a little falling-out, no one knew over what—a gate left open, a tractor left out, an old debt unpaid. But Daddy was by Charles's bed that last day, and Gwynne told me that the brothers clasped hands and held on. It was a death my father later had cause to envy, as his own was to be more protracted and less dignified.

Daddy's strength and sharpness leaked slowly out of him. He began to get lost when he was driving, to call his sisters in the middle of the night. In his late 80's, he was living in Grinnell near Sandy and me in a two-room apartment in a nursing home. He hated it. I hated it for him.

Daddy tried. He tried to be the brave man he was when he and Charles rode the Ladies. He tried to lift himself out of depression, to be glad to see us when we visited. Sandy was wonderful. He spent hours talking to Daddy about old tractors, old friends, a long-ago winning night at the poker table. And the aides loved "Mr. Ferguson," with his courtly Southern manners. Daddy may have lost his strength, but he never lost his appreciation for good-looking women.

One day, Sandy and I found Daddy particularly concerned and agitated. "Charles was here last night," he told us. "I don't know where he went. He needed money, and I couldn't find any to give him. He didn't come to see you, did he?"

We assured him that Charles was all right, both of us realizing that it would be needlessly cruel to remind him that his brother had been dead for over a decade. Gradually, he relaxed, asking Sandy about the mileage on his new truck and the prediction for the corn crop. As we were leaving, though, he said, "He sat in that chair. He didn't stay long."

Daddy saw his brother several times in the following weeks. Sometimes days went by without a visit, and then Charles would be back. Sometimes, Daddy seemed comforted by Charles's presence, but more often, he worried that he hadn't been able to provide some necessity—twenty dollars, food, a place to sleep. On one particularly tense day, Daddy reported that Charles had been sick and sad-looking. "He was kind of stooped over," Daddy said, "and he couldn't get warm. Something was wrong with his hair. He came in that door right there." Daddy pointed to the door to the hall.

Sandy figured it out first. There was a full length mirror on the inside of the door. "How would it be if we taped some paper over that door?" he asked. "It might keep out the draft."

Daddy consented, Sandy went out for butcher's paper and duct tape, and Daddy never saw his brother Charles again.

Thanks:

To Judy Hunter, who got me into this.

To Pamela and Kelly Yenser, for inspiration,
encouragement, and guidance.

To good and patient friends, who have read and
heard these stories, sometimes more than twice.

To my North Carolina cousins Russ, Ben, and Gwynne
Cockman and Tra Perry, who know I tamper with the truth.

To Steve Semken, Natalie Wollenzein,
and the Ice Cube Press.

And to Harley McIlrath, author and editor.

Betty Moffett was born, reared, educated, and married in North Carolina. After four years of teaching high school English and two dramatic years working with the Asolo Theatre in Florida, she, her husband Sandy, and their young son Ruben moved to Grinnell, Iowa, where they planned to stay a year and then return to the sweet sunny South. But they liked the old farm house they fixed up, riding horses in the prairie, teaching at Grinnell College, and playing with the Too Many String Band. Almost five decades later, they're still in Grinnell and glad of it. Betty taught for nearly thirty years in the college's Writing Lab and then began using the advice she offered to her students in her own work. Her stories have appeared in various magazines and journals.

The Ice Cube Press began publishing in 1991 to focus on how to live with the natural world and to better understand how people can best live together in the communities they share and inhabit. Using the literary arts to explore life and experiences in the heartland of the United States we have been recognized by a number of well-known writers including: Gary Snyder, Gene Logsdon, Wes Jackson, Patricia Hampl, Greg Brown, Jim Harrison, Annie Dillard, Ken Burns, Roz Chast, Jane Hamilton, Daniel Menaker, Kathleen Norris, Janisse Ray, Craig Lesley, Alison Deming, Harriet Lerner, Richard Lynn Stegner, Rhodes, Michael Pollan, David Abram, David Orr, and Barry Lopez. We've published a number of well-known authors including: Mary Swander, Jim Heynen, Mary Pipher, Bill Holm, Connie Mutel, John T. Price, Carol Bly, Marvin Bell, Debra Marquart, Ted Kooser, Stephanie Mills, Bill McKibben, Craig Lesley, Elizabeth McCracken, Derrick Jensen, Dean Bakopoulos, Rick Bass, Linda Hogan, Pam Houston, and Paul Gruchow. Check out Ice Cube Press books on our web site, join our email list, facebook group, or follow us on twitter. Visit booksellers, museum shops, or any place you can find good books and support true honest to goodness independent publishing projects so you can discover why we continue striving to "hear the other side."

Ice Cube Press, LLC (est. 1993)
North Liberty, Iowa, Midwest, USA
steve@icecubepress.com
twitter @icecubepress
www.icecubepress.com

to Fenna Marie
and all the stories you have
and will be collecting—
North South East West
High Low Deep & Far ♥